# DATE DUE

## What people are saying about The Boarding House

Marcia Melton has brought us the winning tale of a young girl living under difficult circumstances in Philipsburg, Montana during the early days of the last century. In a series of vignettes, we follow Emmie Hynes as she copes with the struggles of her widowed mother to provide a living for the family while running a boarding house. We learn of the mother's attempts to recover money from the Company for the death of Emmie's father in a mine accident. Emmie follows with enthusiasm the blossoming suffrage movement and joins in admiration of celebrity suffragette, Jeannette Rankin. Emmie's interaction with her brother and other children of her age are beautifully and realistically portrayed.

A wonderful book for any child or adult to read. —Jim Moore, author of *Ride the Jawbone* and *Election Day*

Marcia Melton has created a look back at the lives of 11-year-old Emmie Hynes and her family in the early years of the 20th century for today's young readers in her enjoyable *The Boarding House.* Although the Hynes family has suffered losses and hard times, they also have some exciting and entertaining adventures, and prove once again that doing hard work well and having loving friends is more important than wealth or social standing—a good lesson for young and old alike. —Sue Hart, *Professor, MSU Billings*

A strong setting can make a good story even better. Butte and Philipsburg, Montana fit that criteria. The Boarding House is a story of family and friendship as they face loss and change in 1914 and has a very timeless feel making historical fiction accessible for young readers. —Ellen Crain Butte-*Silver Bow Public Archives.*

The winds of change sweeping through a 1914 drafty boarding

house seek to destroy the fragile support of a young widow and her children following the unnecessary loss of a beloved husband and father.

Conrad, thirteen, is drawn to increasingly undesirable behaviors. Eleven-year-old Emmie, quieter than her red braids, has no idea that she is a younger version of Jeannette Rankin who led the Montana Suffragette Movement giving the vote to Montana Women.

The suspenseful story line is set in the rough mining town of Butte, Montana and the gentler Philipsburg. Marcia Melton is not only intimate with the history of her native Montana, but her fast-paced writing will hold the attention of middle-school readers, and there just might be adults caughts reading it from cover to cover. —Bonnie Buckley Maldonado, author of *From the Marias River to the North Pole and Montana, Too*

The Boarding House is a testament to the perseverance of workers and their families to the perils of early twentieth century copper mining in Butte, Montana. The story follows a widow and her two young children and their struggle to recreate their lives in the nearby mining town of Philipsburg after the tragic death of their husband/father in the Butte mines. The story should be valuable to young readers as a point of comparison to their twentieth century lives. —Brian Shovers, *Librarian, Montana Historical Society*

The Boarding House, by Marcia Melton, is a wonderful work of historical fiction, compelling and well told. By telling a story that both entertains and informs, it serves as an excellent example of the best in historical fiction. The Boarding House allows children to see how history both shapes people and is shaped by them, while also helping children make connections to their own present day lives. —Jaime H. Herrera, *Professor of Children's Literature, Mesa Community College, Arizona*

# The Boarding House

## A Story of Butte and Philipsburg, Montana, 1914

# The Boarding House

Marcia Melton

illustrated by
Fran Doran

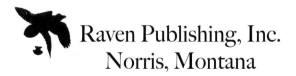

Raven Publishing, Inc.
Norris, Montana

# The Boarding House
ISBN: 978-1-937849-03-0
Published by: Raven Publishing, Inc., PO Box 2866
Norris, MT 59745

Speeches by Jeannette Rankin are taken from: **American Political Women** (Steinman, 1980) and **The Missoulian** (May 3, 1914)

·Copyright © 2012 by Marcia Melton
Cover and inside illustrations © 2012 by Fran Doran
Author photo © 2012 Robin Hickman Photography
Printed in the United States

**Library of Congress Cataloging-in-Publication Data**

Melton, Marcia.
The boarding house / Marcia Melton ; illustrated by Fran Doran.
  p. cm.
 Summary: When their father dies in the copper mines of Butte, Montana, in 1914, eleven-year-old Emmie and her twelve-year-old brother Conrad move with their mother to operate a boarding house in the nearby town of Philipsburg.
 ISBN 978-1-937849-03-0 (trade pbk. : alk. paper) -- ISBN 978-1-937849-04-7 (electronic edition)
[1. Boardinghouses--Fiction. 2. Montana--History--20th century--Fiction.] I. Doran, Fran, ill. II. Title.
 PZ7.M516456Bo 2012
 [Fic]--dc23
                                              2012011079

They had a poster showing two prizefighters and announcing a championship featherweight boxing match in Butte. They danced around the kitchen pretending to box, throwing fake jabs at each other and into the air. Conrad's stocky body absorbed the light punches from Danny, but one caught him off guard. He bumped the cupboard, rattling the dishes.

"You'd better cut it out," Emmie said sternly. "You're going to break something."

Emmie wasn't a very tall girl, and the work of getting the wood from the shed, keeping the stove hot, and boiling water for the dishes was hard. If she had to deal with climbing up on a chair to straighten the dishes in the cupboard or sweep up broken glass, it would be even worse. She wanted the boys out of the kitchen fast. "Get out of here," she said, and she was glad when they slammed the back door.

Conrad lingered at the table after supper that night. "Hey, Em. There's something me and Danny planned for you and Clara," he said.

Emmie looked up doubtfully. Clara was Danny's sister. Emmie had tried to talk to her several times at school, but it didn't work. Clara always stood off by herself, looking suspiciously at everyone. She didn't seem inclined to even want to say hello, much less do something planned by boys.

When Mama came into the dining room to gather the last few dinner dishes off the table, Conrad clammed than Emmie. But when she said that to Conrad, her thin body and her resolve had strength in all the needed places.

Conrad stared down at his shoes.

Emmie wished Conrad didn't feel like a stranger to them. She missed Papa too, and she knew the boarding house was pretty run down, but they were fixing it up more each day. Moving hadn't been easy for any of them, but she thought things were getting better all the time, until Conrad's attitude changed.

Philipsburg wasn't a dump at all. It was smaller and not as exciting as Butte, just different. The mining wasn't done in dangerous underground mines where Papa had worked, but out in the hills where prospectors searched for gold and silver.

Butte was a big booming place, rich in copper way inside the ground and rich in all kinds of people trying to get at that ore. The mile-high city ringed with mountains had mile-high ambitions too.

Philipsburg nestled in the beautiful Flint Creek valley with ranches spread out across the valley floor. Off in the distance were rugged mountains where loggers worked, felling timber. All these jobs brought boarders into town to stay at their boarding house. Couldn't Conrad see that there was more than one good place to live in Montana? Emmie wished Danny would take his tough talk and go right back to Butte.

Conrad showed up later that morning with Danny.

that new kid down the street, Danny Flaherty, moved in, Conrad never had time for anything.

Conrad's moods had been unpredictable last winter after they moved to the boarding house, but just when he seemed to be getting adjusted, Danny showed up. Emmie had a bad feeling about Danny. He and his family had moved to Philipsburg right before school got out. They were from Butte too. Danny talked the Butte tough talk like some kids there and walked with a chip-on-the-shoulder swagger. He tried to act smart by saying bad things about Philipsburg, declaring that as soon as he got old enough, he'd leave this podunk place and go back to Butte to work in the mines.

Maybe it was the Butte talk and that Danny knew all about the mines where Papa had worked, or maybe it was Conrad's newness in Philipsburg, but, somehow, Danny got power over Conrad right away. Conrad had always helped Mama around the boarding house, but now he often left the house, usually with Danny. He acted secretive when Mama asked questions.

Once when Mama had to tell Conrad three times to bring in wood for the stove, he blurted out, "I can't be doin' everything. Let the boarders do it. They boss me around enough. If Papa was here, we'd never have come to this dump anyway."

Mama got tears in her eyes, but she said firmly, "Conrad Hynes, NEVER speak that way again." Sometimes Mama looked like a young girl, not much older

# Chapter One

## The Fight

School had been out for just two weeks. The early summer time of fresh air mornings and fresh air thoughts made everything seem possible. The summer stretched out ahead like a grassy path. As Emmie washed dishes, her brother Conrad tried to slip out the back door before the day's chores were done.

"Where are you going, Connie Hynes?" Emmie demanded.

"If you call me Connie, you'll never know," he said.

That sneaky Conrad, Emmie thought. He can get out of chores faster than butter slips off hot corn. At least calling him Connie was one way to get him. When you're eleven years old, and your home is a boarding house, you have plenty of chores. If your twelve-year-old brother skips out on you, it takes even more of the day to get the jobs done.

"I have to run down to Danny's. It's real important," Conrad said as he twisted the door knob. "I'll be back soon. I'll do a couple extra of your chores then, Em."

Emmie made a face at him. That'll be the day. Since

make-shift Christmas in our sad little house and into January, when Mama told us that we would move across the mountains to a place where she could run a boarding house.

We watched out the windows of the Model T Ford as it slowly chugged up the mountain road past snow banks piled high on either side. A blue sky glistened overhead as we pulled to the top of the hill. Below lay a broad valley and our new home, Philipsburg.

Mama took our mittened hands. "We will start over here, Emmie and Conrad."

My lip shook, but I bit it to make it stop and smiled at my Mama. "I will help you," I said.

This is the story of what happened to us.

Our new home

# Prologue

## A Note from Emmie: Moving to Philipsburg, Montana, 1914

The November day that my Papa died at the mine, I thought the world would end. A cold rain hammered down the streets of Butte, past the tall gallows frames and the rows of miners' houses. It dripped down the windows of the big Anaconda Copper Company building and the Miner's Union Hall, and ran strong in gullies out on the flat land beneath what they called "The Richest Hill on Earth."

By the time our relatives and neighbors filled the parlor that night, the rain had turned to cold sleet and snow. One by one, people came to pay their respects to my Mama as she sat at our kitchen table looking like a fragile leaf. Her green eyes filled with tears over and over again. Her thin shoulders shook. I never left her side and neither did my brother, Conrad. I didn't know what to do to help her, but I knew we had to do something.

The snow piled up higher and higher, through a

*For my mother, Lynn, and my uncle, Warren,
my inspiration for Emmie and Conrad*

Warren Conrad Lovinger & Emma Lynn Lovinger Melton Johnstone

up fast. "Well, it's, um, tomorrow, Em. Don't worry about it now. I'll tell you later," he muttered. He jumped up from the table.

The next day, Saturday, usually meant even more chores. But today Mama had taken the train to Butte, so Emmie finished her jobs early. Conrad bolted out the door at the earliest opportunity. The sounds of the horses and buggies and the putt-putt of the automobile engines on the road in front of the house came in through the open window as the sun warmed the morning. Families from out in the country were in town. The boarding house was near the end of Broadway, Philipsburg's main street. There were lots of voices and things going on outside, but Emmie didn't go out. She took off her apron and smoothed her reddish brown pigtails.

Whenever she had some time to herself, Emmie always chose to do one thing—read. She settled into an overstuffed chair in the parlor. An assortment of chairs, tables, and a sofa that Mama called a settee made the parlor a cozy place. A faded flowered carpet covered most of the wooden floor, scuffed and worn from the work boots of many boarders. When all the grownups were gone, and the house was quiet, Emmie loved this reading place. She opened her book to sink into the world of *Little Women*, but she barely opened the cover when Conrad slammed the back door.

"Emmie," he called out. "Where are you? I've got a great idea for us."

His voice sounded cheery and friendly, something unusual for him these days. Lately, although he looked the same with his wavy, brown hair and elf-like grin, he seemed different, and he never wanted to be bothered with his sister. Maybe the old Conrad was back.

Emmie gladly called out, "I'm in the parlor, Connie." As soon as he came in, she said, "I'm sorry about saying Connie. Sometimes I forget. I promise I'll remember at school." She didn't want to take a chance on his good mood.

"That's okay. I just want to sound grown up, that's all," he said in a burst of rare honesty. He plopped down on the settee, looked thoughtful a minute, then nervous. "Em, I've got a way for us to make some money to buy Mama something really nice for her birthday."

Emmie brightened. "I've been thinking about her birthday, but I don't have a cent. Some money would be great."

"About the thing with Clara. See, Danny thought up the idea that we could put on a show and charge admission, and kids will pay to come see it. We'll split the money. We were thinking you and Clara could be in the show." He squirmed uncomfortably, crossed his arms, and then uncrossed them. He crossed his legs. He looked like a pretzel.

"Me and Clara?"

I've been in some shows before, Emmie thought. We used to do lots of funny little shows for Mama and Papa and at Sunday School and school plays too, but with Clara? She didn't seem like she'd ever sung or danced or recited a poem. She never said a word, just stood to the side of things.

"Clara?" Emmie repeated. "Is it a play or what? Would we sing or talk or what?" She couldn't picture it.

Conrad jumped out of the chair. "Come with me, Em. You'll see. We're setting it up out back. It'll be fun." He was smiling, but there was something not right about it, Emmie thought. The smile was forced and pasted onto his face, but she said, "Okay." It wouldn't hurt to take a quick look.

When they got outside, she could see that it was way more than an idea. Everything was already well underway. Danny and several other boys scurried around the yard, tying a rope to the trees. Clara sat over by the shed looking glum. The rope was tied between two trees and the side of the shed. A barrel made the fourth corner so there was a perfect square. In two corners of the square, across from each other, there were stools from the kitchen with pails of water beside them. Conrad's bathrobe hung over the rope by one stool.

"Is it a play about a boxing match?" Emmie asked.

Conrad quickly replied, "Yep, that's it, Em. A play about a boxing match."

Danny walked over and said, "Mr. Hynes, I see you're here for the big fight." He looked menacingly at Emmie. That scrawny little Danny was trying to act like some sort of big shot. The poster from the Butte champion-ship featherweight match was nailed to a tree.

All of a sudden, Emmie realized what was really hap-pening. All these kids. A boxing ring. Kids placing bets. The air was thick with trouble, and Mama was gone.

Conrad had her by the arm. A bunch of boys ran over to stand around the ring.

In a loud voice that sounded like the man from the circus in Butte, Danny bellowed, "Tickets. Have your tickets ready, folks. Place your bets right here."

Emmie heard a boy say, "Clara's big. Conrad's sister is so skinny. This is gonna be good!" Her mind raced. Boxing? Clara? She tried to pull away to run back to the house, but Conrad dragged her along.

"Let me go!" She struggled to get free, but Con-rad held tight. He glanced nervously at Danny and the crowd. "Everybody's here. Come on. For Mama."

It flashed through Emmie's mind that this wasn't for Mama at all. And this wasn't the old Conrad either, but the Conrad stranger—bamboozled by Danny, giving a phony smile to the crowd, trying to lead Emmie to the ring, and squeezing her arm too tightly.

"Let loose of me!" Emmie struggled with all her might to yank free, but Conrad wouldn't let go. He ma-neuvered her to the corner and tried to drape his bath-robe over her shoulders.

"Get this off of me!" Emmie shook and the bathrobe fell on the ground.

Danny was in the center of the ring as he called out in his slick promoter voice, "And now, ladies and gentlemen, in the right corner, Killer Clara Flaherty, all the way from Butte, Montana. And in the left corner, right here from our own Philipsburg, Montana, the bantam weight, Emmie 'The Mouse' Hynes."

Cheers went up around the ring. Emmie heard a boy laughing. "Mouse is right. This'll be over fast."

Bang! Danny hit a silver pail with a shovel. "Round One."

Before she could get away, Danny came over and pushed Emmie into the ring. Clara jumped up with a little hop, her hands punching the air. She headed straight for Emmie.

Emmie glanced frantically around the ring trying to find a way to get out. She heard Conrad yell, "Duck, Emmie. Put your hands up!"

Clara punched her in the arm. It stung, and she stepped backwards. Clara moved in and socked her again, this time in the stomach. The air went out of Emmie, and she thought she'd fall over. Clara lunged forward, punching into thin air. When she didn't connect with Emmie, she lost her balance and fell onto her knees.

Bang! The shovel hit the pail. "End of Round One," Danny yelled out.

Emmie swayed as she tried to see which way to go. Conrad stood uneasily by the stool. "Good start, Em. You're doin' fine. Dance around her," he said in his fakey voice, designed for the nearby spectators to hear. He patted both of her cheeks with his hands.

Emmie felt dizzy. Her arm ached, and she thought she might throw up from the stomach punch. She stared in stunned disbelief at Conrad as he shoved a drink of water at her.

"Emmie," Conrad said in a strained voice. "Come on. Fight."

"Round Two," announced Danny.

Shaking her head and trying to focus her eyes as she stood up, Emmie saw blood stains near the bottom of Clara's dress. Her stockings drooped down and blood ran down her leg from one knee. Emmie put her hands up and moved out of range a couple of times. Whenever she did, Clara turned, and Emmie had to move again. She managed to escape any blows until suddenly, WHAM. Clara landed a hard blow to Emmie's left shoulder. Emmie went right down to the ground and banged her head.

"End of Round Two," Danny yelled.

Conrad leapt into the middle of the ring to help Emmie up. Her head wobbled worse than the last time. She collapsed onto the stool. Through her confusion, she heard a few boys around the ring chanting, "Clar-a. Clar-a."

"Emmie!" Conrad splashed water onto her face. "Look alive, Em. Fight back!" He looked desperate.

Emmie shook her head. Everything was blurry and

out of focus. She thought she might fall off the stool. One of her pigtails was undone, and her hair hung over her eye. She had to get away somehow, but there was no way out of the ring. She cried, "No, no."

"You've got to fight back," Conrad said desperately.

Then all of a sudden, something snapped in Emmie. From somewhere came a surge of fight-back power. It started small and grew fast. She stood up. "OK, Buster. I will fight back. I'll fight you, Conrad Hynes, and I'll fight Clara too and Danny too."

"Round Three," Danny yelled.

Emmie entered the ring, hopping on one foot and then the other. The pain in her arm was gone. The blurriness and shock were gone. She only wanted to get out there and punch Clara.

She got to the center of the ring before Clara, who staggered out slowly, looking dazed. Emmie delivered a few punches. Still, Clara didn't budge. Hitting her felt like hitting a brick wall. Emmie stayed steady, her arms up, moving into position, until one solid jab connected with Clara's right shoulder. Her next punch went off into thin air, but then she got Clara in the left arm. Emmie was a lightning bolt. Conrad cheered. The crowd whooped in surprised excitement.

The tide had turned. Emmie surged forward until she heard Clara say, "OW," really loudly. Suddenly, there was no stopping Clara. She went wild. Emmie tried to get out of the way, but it seemed like Clara had four pairs of hands, all punching at Emmie. Blows rained down like hailstones from every direction. Emmie put her hands over her head. She couldn't get her breath.

"Connie!" she cried out in desperation. She knew she would go down any minute. Then she'd have to deal with Clara from the ground.

At that moment, Emmie heard a loud voice through the noise of the jeering boys. "What's going on here?" a man's voice yelled. "Stop! NOW!"

Old Nels Arnesson, one of the men who lived at their boarding house, grabbed the rope that was tied to the tree, jerking it loose. He strode into the center of the ring. "What is this?" His booming voice would have stopped a freight train.

The cheering faded to an uneasy silence. Conrad stood fixed to his spot by the stool, barely breathing. His panicked eyes glanced toward Emmie. Danny backed up against the shed. The crowd of boys moved away from the ring, looking nervously at each other.

Old Nels looked at Conrad first. "Don't you move," he barked. "You either," he growled at Danny.

Clara stood motionless. "Sit down," Nels said, motioning her to the stool.

Kneeling down, he helped Emmie up. "Oh, my," he murmured, pulling a handkerchief out of his pocket to wipe her bloody lip and chin. Her right eye was swollen shut, and her lip puffed out.

"It'll be okay now," Nels said and helped her to a

patch of shade by a tree. "Sit down here and hold this cloth on your chin. I'll be back in a minute." He patted her on the head.

Nels gave Conrad and Danny a look of steel and commanded, "Stay right there."

He banished the remaining crowd. "Now you kids, get out of here." He motioned to a few stragglers still lurking near the side of the yard, hoping to see the next stage of the day's action—Conrad and Danny's punishment. "Way out of here!"

He turned to the two former fight promoters. "You two get into the shed until I figure out what's going on here. And stay there." Conrad and Danny quickly made their way to the shed like shadows and disappeared into its musty darkness.

Clara stared at the whole scene, looking dazed. "Are you all right?" Nels asked her. Clara nodded her head slightly as Nels motioned to her to follow him.

Emmie opened her one good eye and squinted through the swollen one. Nels walked toward her with Clara sullenly plodding behind him.

"Tell me what happened here, girls," Nels said. His Swedish accent sounded soft and gruff at the same time.

Clara looked down at the ground. Emmie said, in a very small voice, "The boys made us fight." Her voice quivered and tears stung her eyes.

"Is that it?" Nels asked Clara. She nodded again as

she had before. She didn't look at Emmie or Nels.

"Well, it's over now," Nels said. "It was wrong, and the boys will be punished. You girls need to know that this is no way to act. This is the end of it, and you are not to finish this fight. Ever. Just because the boys made you fight doesn't mean you can't get along and be friends. I want you girls to shake hands now."

Emmie's arm hurt so badly that she didn't think she could lift it. When she did, it shook. She reached up, and Clara, still looking down at her shoes, put her hand out too. They didn't really shake, just touched fingers. Clara gave a small nod, and Emmie whispered, "I'm sorry, Clara." She knew Clara wouldn't say "I'm sorry" back, but that didn't matter. What Emmie was sorry for was that it had happened—and maybe a little bit that she'd felt happy when Clara said, "Ow." Fighting was a bad thing. It made a person be what they didn't want to be.

"Do you want to go home or stay here?" Nels asked Clara. "I can take you home."

Clara shook her head, turned around, and started slowly across the yard. Even though Clara had just beaten her to a pulp, Emmie felt sad for her. She wondered what Clara's mother would say, or if she'd even be there, or if she'd even notice.

"Now, little one," Nels bent down to help Emmie up. "Let's get you cleaned up."

Emmie tried to smile with her puffed-up lips. She ached all over. She longed to see Mama.

Finally, when it was almost suppertime, Mama got home. When Emmie saw Mama, a tear dripped out of her eye. Mama put her arms around Emmie and said, "Oh, my darling."

Mama was like the calm, clear pools in the stream behind the boarding house. Just the sound of her voice and her soft touch could smooth Emmie out and make things seem all right.

The boys were in the shed all afternoon. Nels went in once and then left the culprits alone to contemplate their doom. Emmie never did know exactly what he'd said to the boys, but they looked awful when they finally came out of the shed.

Mama's disappointment and distress at her son was so deep it could go right down to the center of the earth. She shook her head and frowned. Her lips were a thin line.

Conrad was a sorry looking sight. Danny looked shifty-eyed and not very sorry.

While Mama, Emmie, Nels, and a few of the boarders who had gotten home from work looked on, Conrad and Danny took down the ring, put the stools and other things back, and removed the poster. They had to throw the poster away. It took a few uncomfortable moments before Danny could reluctantly release the poster from his fingers. Then he slammed it into the barrel. When everything was cleared up, they went into the parlor where the boys were to apologize. Emmie sat on the settee. Mama, Nels, and the boarders looked very serious.

Danny kept his eyes fixed on the floor and barely muttered, "Sorry," under his breath.

Conrad looked right into Emmie's eyes. "I did wrong. I'm…" His voice cracked, and his chin went right down to his chest.

Mama reached out and put her hand on his shoulder. He looked up again. His face was all blotchy. He took a long and shaky sniff. Danny looked at Conrad in disbelief.

Conrad's shoulders shuddered, and he blurted out, "I'm sorry, Em. Really sorry."

Just like with Clara, even though the whole fight thing had happened, right then, Emmie felt bad for Conrad. "It's okay, Connie," she said. "It's over now."

Mama and Nels walked down the street to Flaherty's house with Conrad and Danny marching along in tow. Emmie had heard that Mr. Flaherty used a belt to punish his children. She didn't want to think of it. She sank into the fluffy pillow on the sofa. All she wanted was for everything to come back to normal. For Conrad to be his old self. For Mama not to worry. And, if the truth be known, for her not to miss Papa every minute. But, she'd settle for a new normal right now—and never to be in a boxing match again.

# Chapter Two

## Mama's Birthday

It took a while for the hubbub to die down after the fight. Though no one mentioned it outright, an uneasy feeling hung in the air. Emmie's black eye was a constant reminder. But after a few days, the eye faded to a greenish yellow along with the raw memories of the fight.

Conrad became a model of helpfulness, which Emmie regarded as close to a miracle. Danny stayed out of sight, which was a good thing because if he'd shown up at the door, Old Nels and the other boarders would have probably chased him all the way back down Broadway. Conrad didn't leave the house all week. Emmie didn't ask, but she figured that was part of the punishment.

At the end of the touchy week, Emmie finally broke the ice by asking Conrad to help her plan Mama's birthday party. He quickly replied, "Anything you want, Emmie. Just anything."

Mama's birthday was the next Friday. Emmie and Conrad decided to have a surprise party for her. They had to tell Mama that they would have a cake on Saturday, but they didn't let on about the party.

"That's good," Mama agreed. "I won't have to add another year for one more day." She smiled, but there was sadness in her eyes. Emmie knew this sad smile so well. It was Mama's pretending-everything-is-fine look.

This was the first birthday celebration without Papa, who had always made birthdays, especially Mama's, so much fun. He would sing in his rich Irish voice and dance them around the kitchen, his dark eyes twinkling and his deep, cheery laugh filling the room. Emmie would stand on Papa's feet with her arms around his waist, sandwiched in between her parents while they danced. It was the best place in the world to be. Emmie resolved to do everything in her power to give Mama even a tiny bit of happiness on her birthday.

Saturday was a good time for the party because the boarding house didn't serve Saturday supper. Most of the boarders went down to the saloon that night to drink and play cards, but a few of the boarders who didn't go out, like Old Nels or Tom Beam, stayed home to play a game of charades in the parlor and eat popcorn. On these Saturday nights, the boarding house filled with friendly laughter. Old Nels was especially funny playing charades. He still didn't know some English words, even though he'd come from Sweden many years ago. In charades, his pale blue eyes would squint, and when he'd finally get the word, he'd laugh the best laugh and say, "You got me that time for sure!" On Saturday nights, Emmie sometimes saw Mama's smile seem more carefree like it always was before Papa died. Emmie planned that they would play charades at the party.

Besides Old Nels and Tom Beam, the other guests she would invite to the party were Emmie's new best friend, Dorothy Lovelace, and her mother. Mrs. Lovelace had asked Mama to a suffrage meeting a few weeks ago, and Emmie hoped Mama might find a friend too. Emmie also invited their elderly neighbors, Mr. and Mrs. Taylor, and the owner of the boarding house, Miss Ruth Davies, and her friend, Miss Belle, from Anaconda.

Emmie had planned the guest list carefully before inviting everyone so there would be plenty of places to sit in the parlor, but she surprised herself by inviting more than the parlor would seat. When she had gone to invite Mr. and Mrs. Taylor, she ran into Clara, trudging along with a big bag of potatoes and a squirming baby on her hip. Emmie started to hurry by with a quick nod when Clara blurted out, "Wait, Emmie, I wanted to tell you, I'm sorry about... everything." Clara looked hesitant.

Emmie knew that speaking took courage for Clara. "It's okay, Clara. It's over now." All of a sudden she heard herself ask, "Would you like to come to my Mama's birthday party next Saturday?"

Clara looked so surprised that Emmie thought she might drop the baby. "Really? Well, sure, Emmie. Yes." Clara's smile was pretty. Emmie had never seen it.

"You could bring your Mama too...and the baby too," Emmie said. As she walked away, she could hardly believe her own ears that she'd done this, but at that moment, it just popped out. Clara probably didn't get invited to very many parties.

Everyone planned presents for Mama. Even Tom Beam, their grizzled old boarder who worked at the mill, bought Mama a lace handkerchief from Mrs. Elizabeth McDonel's Millinery Shop in Philipsburg. Emmie pictured the unlikely scene of Tom in the ladies' shop, standing at the glass-topped counter, asking the fancy clerk to see the snowy white handkerchiefs, and picking one with his rough, cracked hands.

Trying to get back in everyone's good graces with a special birthday gift, Conrad had the idea of transplanting wild shooting star flowers from up on the hill into pots for the kitchen windowsill. They looked pretty with their dainty pink flowers bending down slightly. Conrad wanted to please Mama so much that he had three pots already planted and was planning more. It seemed like Conrad might move the whole hillside into the kitchen.

Nels's present was a small wooden box that he made for Mama. He was always building and carving things, so Mama didn't suspect anything when she saw him working with his knife on a piece of wood. When he showed it to Emmie and Conrad, they rubbed their fingers over the lid to feel its perfect smoothness. He had carved a simple "H" into it.

Mama's name was Honora. Honora Grady Hynes.

Emmie thought it was the perfect name for her. Mama was the most honorable person in the world.

Emmie was making Mama an apron from the cloth left over from the bedroom curtains. The cloth had dainty blue flowers on a white background. Emmie hoped to trim the pocket with lace. Mama wore her apron most of the day every day except when she went out of the house. A new one would be a good present. Dorothy and her mother offered sewing help.

Ever since Valentine's Day, when Dorothy had invited Emmie to a party, the two girls were an inseparable pair, the tall, blonde, curly-haired Dorothy and the little freckle-nosed Emmie with her thick braids. They spent as much time together as they could, but this week Emmie was at Dorothy's all afternoon every day. She was gone so much that Mama finally said, "Emmie, I miss you in the afternoons. Wouldn't you like to invite Dorothy over here?"

"Next week," Emmie said, hoping her answer would satisfy Mama.

Even though the stitches were a little uneven, Emmie loved to look at the apron as it took shape. The top bib and ties were sewn on, but she still had to do the hem and pocket.

On Saturday morning, Mama was up early to get breakfast for the boarders. Emmie rubbed her eyes as she came into the warm kitchen. Outside the window, the sky turned from dark to gray-blue. Mama always got up before daylight, so she had a candle burning on the work table in the center of their roomy kitchen. She said it was to light the way from darkness to a new day. The kitchen smelled good, with aromas of bacon, baked bread, and coffee all blended together.

Mama put down her spatula and wrapped her arm around Emmie's shoulders. "What would I do without my morning partner?" she said.

Emmie knew that a lot of girls at her school whose families lived in the bigger houses off Broadway Street were still asleep in their fluffy beds, but she didn't mind having to get up so early. All the boarders said their breakfasts were the best west of the Continental Divide—and probably east of it too!

Emmie noticed Mama's sad eyes today. She wished she'd gotten up even earlier to keep her company. This birthday was going to be a hard one for her. "Happy Birthday," Emmie said as she hugged Mama tight around the waist.

Breakfast took forever as the boarders lingered over coffee. Emmie grew more and more anxious, thinking of the unfinished apron at Dorothy's house and the preparations needed for the surprise party.

Conrad acted nervous too. When Mama mentioned that this afternoon she might go out to the shed to begin some summer gardening, he looked panicked. He had his entire wildflower potting project set up in the shed.

Emmie whizzed through finishing the dishes and

hurriedly did her chores. Finding Mama in the parlor, she said as casually as possible, "I think I'll mosey up to Dorothy's."

She zoomed out the door, down the street, around the corner, up the hill, and arrived breathlessly on Dorothy's doorstep.

Dorothy opened the door. "At last you're here, Em," she exclaimed. "The apron is on the dining room table."

Mrs. Lovelace came down the curved staircase into the wood-paneled dining room. "Hello, dear. Today's the day for the final touches."

Emmie nodded. "I need to hurry. I've got so much left to do." She sat down at the table, threaded her needle, and started right in on the hem.

At first the stitches were even, but the more she hurried, the more uneven they became. Dorothy and her mother went into the kitchen and Emmie sat alone at the polished dining room table. She decided to take out the last few stitches she had done and start over. The hem bunched up. She hurried the stitches, but the thread knotted, and she had to stop to untangle it.

The gold grandfather clock in the hall chimed twelve noon. The Lovelaces' home was so nice with its thick rugs and fancy furniture, but today the whole house felt like a giant clock, ticking closer to the time for the party. The distance to the end of the apron hem looked very far from the place where Emmie struggled with her uneven stitches. She hadn't even started on the pocket yet.

With every tick of the clock and stitch of the needle, Emmie's stomach tied in more of a knot. When the thread tangled up again for about the tenth time, her eyes filled with tears. The tears dripped onto the apron, and the needle wouldn't go through the wet spots on the cloth. Her nose started to run, and she wiped it with her hand. Then she forgot and wiped her hand on the apron. She hung her head and stared at the crumpled heap of bunched cloth and puckered thread in her hands.

Suddenly Mrs. Lovelace and Dorothy were on either side of her. "Emmie, darling, what happened?" Mrs. Lovelace took the cloth from her hands. "We can fix it."

Emmie could only squeak out, "It's getting all messed up. I want it to be so nice. I just want her to be happy for her birthday."

Mrs. Lovelace put the apron on the table and gently gathered Emmie into her arms. Emmie leaned against Mrs. Lovelace and cried. Dorothy patted Emmie's shoulder. They all knew that these tears were not just about the apron.

After a while, Emmie stopped crying, and Mrs. Lovelace said softly, "You are doing everything possible for your Mama."

"Maybe the party will help," Emmie whispered.

"It will," Dorothy said. "I know it will." That was one of the best things about Dorothy. She always found the bright side.

"OK now, girls." Mrs. Lovelace said, smoothing the apron out on the table. "We don't have much time left. Emmie, you keep stitching from this end. I will hem from the other end, and we'll meet in the middle. Dorothy, you get a hot iron ready so we can iron out these wrinkles. We may have to skip the pocket though," she said cautiously.

"I know," Dorothy chimed in, "you can just tell her about it and sew it on later."

With a shaky smile, Emmie picked up her needle. In no time at all, the apron was hemmed and pressed. She had started with only a piece of curtain cloth, and now it was an apron. She wanted to sit holding and admiring it for a long time, but there wasn't a minute to spare. The time for the party was looming dangerously close.

"Let's wrap up the apron, and then you run home quickly, dear," Mrs. Lovelace said.

"Wait. I'll go with you," Dorothy said eagerly.

"Good idea." Mrs. Lovelace got out some tissue paper for wrapping the present. After the apron was neatly folded into a square package, she ushered the girls out the door. "Run along. I'll join you when it's time for the party."

When the girls got to the boarding house, they found a note on the table from Mama to say she had gone down the street to the grocery store.

"Whew," Emmie gasped. "We need time to set things up."

The party was scheduled for late afternoon. Emmie and Conrad had made a plan with Nels to get Mama out of the house so all the guests could assemble for the surprise. Now they had to rearrange their plan.

Conrad and Nels quickly took off down the street to intercept Mama and keep her away from the house a while longer. The girls spread a fresh pressed tablecloth on the table and put the chairs around the parlor.

Emmie was especially eager to see Miss Davies and her friend Belle. Since employing the Hynes family to run the boarding house for her, Miss Davies had fallen in love with this little family from Butte. She didn't have any family of her own left in this world so she said she would be their honorary aunt. Emmie and Conrad called her Auntie Ruthie. She didn't get to come to see them very often because she was getting up in years and getting low on money, but today she and Belle were driving over from Anaconda in Belle's Model T Ford. Belle was even older than Ruth. Not many women drove cars, and certainly not ones as old as Belle and Ruth, but they were adventurous. "Why, if men can drive cars, then so can we," they exclaimed. "We'll come over in the Tin Lizzie."

The Tin Lizzie was an open to the air coupe, with black leather seats, a steering wheel on a long shaft, and wheels with spindly spokes. Emmie kept glancing out the window to see them pull up, and finally, just as Emmie and Dorothy were starting to set the table, the Tin

Lizzie sputtered to a stop out front. The two ladies were perched in the seats like well-feathered birds. They wore floppy hats as if to disguise themselves in case they saw Mama as they drove into town.

"The coast is clear," Emmie called as she waved them in the door.

"Wonderful," Ruthie and Belle exclaimed, bustling into the parlor, their arms full with bags and treats. Ruthie carried a luscious three-layer cake with gleaming white frosting.

The girls and Ruthie and Belle were in the middle of scurrying to arrange things on the table when they heard Mama, Conrad, and Nels come in the back door. Nels's hearty laugh warned them that they'd been found out.

"I think we're here a little too soon, but Happy Birthday to you!" he chuckled as Mama discovered the surprise in the dining room. "The kids have made a big party for you."

Mama put her hands on her cheeks. "My goodness!" she said incredulously. "What a surprise!"

"Rootie!" Nels gave Auntie Ruthie a big hug. She'd been his landlady for many years. The party had started.

Mrs. Lovelace appeared next at the door. Mama shook Mrs. Lovelace's hand. "How nice of you to come."

Mr. and Mrs. Taylor arrived from down the street. Right behind them were Clara and her mother. Clara's mother held the baby in her arms and a small bouquet of lilacs in her hand. Danny lurked behind them. Mama, Conrad, and Emmie were all at the door in an instant.

"Please come in. We're glad you're here," Mama said welcomingly.

Clara stood back until Emmie moved toward her and said, "Hi, Clara. Come on in." Clara wore a blue dress, and a bow hung crookedly in her hair. It was the first time Emmie had ever seen anything resembling a bow on any part of Clara. Mrs. Flaherty stayed just outside the door. She looked young and tired. When she saw the roomful of people, she hesitated, but Mama quickly beckoned her inside to introduce her around the room. Everyone fussed over the chubby-cheeked baby. Mrs. Flaherty spoke softly with an Irish accent, "Happy Birthday, Mrs. Hynes. Thank you for inviting us, Emmie."

Emmie had confessed to Conrad about her spontaneous invitation to Clara and that Danny might be bold enough to show up too. Emmie thought he would because there was cake involved.

Conrad was prepared and said, "Hi, Danny, sit over there," motioning to the corner where Danny wouldn't be too much in the sight of Old Nels.

When Tom Beam came downstairs, the party was complete. Everyone talked together about the weather and the coming summer. The children listened patiently to the chatting until at last, Auntie Ruthie lit the candles on the cake, and they all sang "Happy Birthday." Mama blew out all of the thirty-five candles.

The cake was so good that Emmie, Dorothy, Conrad, Clara, and Danny all asked for seconds, and Auntie Ruthie's seconds were bigger than firsts. It wasn't often that a fancy cake like this was served at the boarding house.

When it was time to open the presents, Emmie placed them all around Mama's chair. She was always the slowest person at opening presents, and Emmie knew she would make a nice fuss over each one.

Mrs. Lovelace and Dorothy brought a box of candy from Gamers Candies in Butte. Emmie recognized the shiny box right away. That store had what looked like a mile of glass cases with something fabulous on every tray. When they lived in Butte, Papa used to bring home treats from there. As Mama held the Gamers box in her hands, Emmie knew she was thinking of Papa.

When Conrad brought in all his flower pots, everyone laughed as he carried in one after another. Tom smiled shyly when Mama opened the handkerchief. Nels chuckled when she marveled over his lovely wooden box.

Each time Mama reached for a present, Emmie hoped she would pick the square flat one wrapped in tissue paper. At last, she opened it. Emmie held her breath.

"Emmie, this is beautiful," Mama exclaimed. "You made it." She held up the apron and turned it over and over. "And look, a pocket." The pocket fell out of the wrapping.

"I'm going to sew it on tomorrow," Emmie quickly explained. "I ran out of time."

"Oh, no, you didn't, my Emmie," Mama said. "It's the prettiest apron I've ever seen."

Mrs. Lovelace and Dorothy both winked at Emmie. Mama tied the apron around her waist and wore it for the rest of the party. The party went on and on until a few people said that they must go home for supper.

After the other guests had gone home, Auntie Ruthie bustled into the kitchen to prepare the dinner. She'd brought meat-stuffed pasties, Nels's favorite. "Good thing we're staying the night, Belle. The tires would go flat if we got into the car after all this food," Ruthie teased.

After dinner they played charades. Mama still wore her apron, and Belle and Ruthie put on their floppy hats again. Between Auntie Ruthie and Nels trying to guess the acts and the floppy hats bobbing sideways with the actions, the game was interrupted over and over as laughter filled the parlor and echoed up the stairs. They all wanted the good feelings to go on and on.

It was almost midnight when Emmie's eyes finally started to droop. Conrad yawned, and Mama said, "I guess we must turn in. It was a wonderful party."

Their lives had changed so much since they lost their handsome Papa. They were all trying so hard to make the best of things even though they missed him all the time. Today they had made it through another milestone, Mama's birthday. If only he could have been with them, Emmie thought as she snuggled down into her bed. Still, they had made it a good day for Mama and Emmie knew that was what Papa would want.

And maybe, just maybe, the old Conrad was back too.

# Chapter Three

## Columbia Gardens

A few weeks after the birthday party, Mr. and Mrs. Lovelace and Dorothy invited Mama, Emmie, and Conrad to go to Butte for a noon picnic at a rally for the upcoming election about women's voting rights and a horse race in the afternoon. All this in one day and with Dorothy and her parents—to Emmie, it seemed too good to be true. She could hardly wait, but a small hesitation crept into her mind.

This would be her and Conrad's first trip back to their old town since they moved to Philipsburg. Mama had been back several times, once on the fateful day of Emmie's fight with Clara. Emmie didn't like to think about that day.

When Mama went to Butte, it was to meet with a lawyer and other families from the Miners' Union, trying to get settlements of money from accidents at the mines. She came home discouraged each time. The mine conditions were horribly unsafe and the mine owners were rich, but when accidents like Papa's happened and the workers and their families suffered, the mining company always found a way out of paying for the tragedies.

It was hard on Mama to have to fight for money that was rightfully theirs, and on the days when she had to go to Butte, she always came home worn and discouraged. Emmie hoped today would be a day of fun and not sad memories.

All of the events were being held at Columbia Gardens, a large park on the edge of Butte. It was one good thing the wealthy man who owned the mining company had done for the people of Butte. "The Gardens" had lawns of thick green grass and bright beds of flowers, a spacious Pavilion with a big dance floor and a wide veranda, an ice cream parlor, a musical carousel, a gigantic white wooden roller coaster, and a race track. In the rough, tough mining town of Butte, Columbia Gardens was a world apart, a place for families to meet and play. Emmie remembered going there last summer with Papa and Mama. Now that seemed like a long time ago —but sometimes it seemed like just yesterday.

As they pulled out of Philipsburg, the air was brisk. The sun shone on the Lovelaces' shiny black touring car. Everyone was dressed in their best clothes, and Mrs. Lovelace had brought blankets for them to put over their laps until the morning sun warmed the day. Mama told Emmie to wear her yellow pinafore because yellow, white, gold, and purple were the colors the suffragettes, the ladies working for the vote, wore. Mama wore a pretty white blouse, a black skirt, and a wide-brimmed hat with a gold ribbon band on it in support of suffrage.

Emmie felt dressed for Sunday in her yellow pinafore and black lace-up shoes. They squeezed her toes, but she didn't tell Mama. Money for new lace-up shoes would be hard to find. They weren't so important in summer anyway, and maybe her feet wouldn't grow much by September when school started. Emmie's hair was tightly braided, but no matter how tight Mama got it, some strands of wispy hair always escaped. She had scrubbed her face this morning until it shone like the sun.

The dirt road was bumpy along the way to Butte, and they were crowded together in the car. As they bumped along the ruts, uphill and down, Mrs. Lovelace and Mama talked about the voting issue and Mr. Lovelace chimed in from time to time. Mama had been telling Emmie about the importance of the upcoming election in November. The election would decide whether or not women would get to vote in Montana.

Mrs. Lovelace explained that the main speaker at the rally would be Miss Jeannette Rankin from Missoula. "She is so young to be the leader of the people in Montana who are working to get voting rights for women. I hear that she's a wonderful speaker, and she has big dreams to become a political leader in Washington someday too."

Anticipation filled the car for everyone: for Mrs. Lovelace and Mama, a rally to support their hopes for voting rights; for Mr. Lovelace, a horse race; and for the children squeezed happily into the backseat, Columbia Gardens and a whole day of fun.

But as they pulled into Butte, a silence fell in the car. Driving past the rows and rows of ramshackle miners' houses brought forth so many memories for the Hynes family. The memories surrounded them like fog, replacing their eager anticipation with wordless remembering. Mr. and Mrs. Lovelace and Dorothy were quiet too.

Emmie had thought it would be fun to see Butte again, but it wasn't. As she looked out the window at their old neighborhood in Dublin Gulch, her thoughts went back to the days in their old house. Right back to the day when a man had arrived at their door and told them that a hoist at the mine had gone out of control, dropping the wire cage deep into the mine. Their wonderful, strong, beloved Papa was dead. As if it had been only a moment ago, Emmie remembered Mama saying, "No, no," and sinking to the floor as if her body was crushed too.

Memories of that time and the awful weeks following it had softened in Emmie's mind as their new life took hold in Philipsburg. Seeing Butte again brought it all flooding back. In those days, when they lived in shadows as they tried to go on without Papa, Emmie and Conrad hardly left Mama's side. Conrad became a quiet ghost in the house instead of the rough-and-tumble Butte boy he had been. Emmie felt lonely and worried all the time. To keep them going, Mama had taken in sewing and cleaned houses for rich people. She grew thinner and thinner until her dresses hung on her like they were hanging on a clothes hanger instead of a person. Emmie had often snuggled into Mama's bed at night, wanting to be near her and hold onto her, afraid that Mama might let go of life too. The memories gave Emmie a chill. Maybe they shouldn't have come today, she thought. Maybe they would backslide and lose all the progress they'd made in Philipsburg.

As they drove into downtown Butte, Mr. and Mrs. Lovelace and Dorothy gently started the conversation. Dorothy pointed to the candy store. "There's Gamers."

"And Hennessy's Department Store," Mrs. Lovelace added. "Look at those windows of summer dresses."

"Whoa, trolley car comin'," Mr. Lovelace said as the streetcar rattled by, bells clanging to move traffic out of the way. "No time for shopping now. Have to get these ladies to the rally. Can't miss hearing Miss Jeannette Rankin, the lioness of Montana suffrage."

Butte seemed huge to Emmie now. It had blocks and blocks of a bustling downtown with buildings several stories high and glittering shop windows. The streets were crowded with people of every description. Rough-looking miners bumped up against bowler-hatted businessmen, and fancy ladies tripped along the sidewalk in long skirts and high-heeled shoes. Paper boys shouted from the corners, waving the Butte Miner and Standard newspapers at passersby.

In Butte the big, fancy, rich people's houses were near the downtown. The miners' houses clung to the steep hillsides leading up to the mines and spilled into the gulches and gullies like puzzle pieces all jumbled together. Each group of miners' houses was a neighborhood with a name and identity all its own: Centerville, Muckerville, Cabbage Patch, Corktown, Parrot Flat, and Dublin Gulch.

Philipsburg's main street was wide and dusty with a mercantile, a bank, a livery stable, and small shops. At one end of town stood their boarding house, a two-story, rough-sided, brown building with big double doors, a second-story front balcony, and a sign that read ROOMS. It didn't look like a regular home, but to them it was. Up the hilly side streets were brick and frame houses with flowers in the yards and rocking chairs on the porches. In only six months of living there, Emmie knew who lived in many of the houses. She hadn't thought so clearly about the differences between Butte and Philipsburg until today.

They cheered up in the bustle of downtown Butte and were pointing out interesting sights in the streets when Mrs. Lovelace startled them by saying loudly, "Edwin, turn right here! Let's avoid the Miners' Union Hall area."

"Good idea," Mr. Lovelace replied quickly, turning the corner so sharply that they all slid across the seat in a heap.

As they drove up the road to Columbia Gardens, Mr. Lovelace cleared his throat and said seriously, "Children, you might as well know this. Someone has dynamited the Miners' Union Hall and there's been a fire and lots of fighting. There's trouble between the mine bosses and the workers over wages and working conditions—the same things your good mother is fighting for. Butte is a dangerous place these days. Today should be a great day at the Gardens, but if any trouble breaks out, we'll have to head home to Philipsburg early. Don't wander too far away from us."

"Thank you," Mama said. "There is so much trouble over the mines these days. Sometimes it almost seems as if Butte might split apart."

Emmie and Conrad knew about mining troubles. Many nights in their little kitchen in Dublin Gulch, Papa and other men had discussed how to win fair wages and safe working conditions from the mine bosses. Mama now struggled with the same problems. Even after his death, Papa still stood for fairness as Mama worked with the other families to get payments for the men injured and killed doing mining work.

Mr. Lovelace continued the mine discussion with Mrs. Lovelace and Mama. Dorothy gave Emmie a grimace that meant "Once this talking is over, we'll be able to get out of the car and have some fun." Conrad fidgeted in his seat.

"It's a crime. Look at this place! Generosity on one

hand and criminal disregard on the other," Mr. Lovelace said, waving his hand and pointing to the gardens. "All money and profits. Not that the old owners, the ones they called the Copper Kings, were all good, but it was different before. Now it's all for the company. I don't think there'd be a Columbia Gardens if it hadn't been built before these new bosses." He was getting so worked up that he motored past several available parking places.

Emmie had one ear tuned to the grownups' conversation, wondering how the mining company could build these big gardens and not have any money to help families of the workers.

Mama spoke hesitantly, "It's hard to fight them for what's right, but I can't give up hope that there may be some changes coming. You are so kind to bring us here today. Thank you."

"It's your bravery, Mrs. Hynes," Mrs. Lovelace said. "We admire you so much. My goodness…, we want to help you and the children…. My lands, what can I say." For once, Mrs. Lovelace was at a loss for words.

Mr. Lovelace pulled to a stop. "Glad to be here indeed," he announced with a flourish, trying to lighten the grownups' mood. He opened the car door. The ladies smoothed themselves from the dusty ride as Dorothy, Emmie, and Conrad scrambled out of the back seat and jumped off the running board.

They all carried the baskets of food they had brought over to one of the picnic tables under the trees. The wide green lawns of Columbia Gardens stretched out before them. Over by the Pavilion, women bustled about lining up chairs in front of a stage on the lawn. Bright purple and gold banners reading "VOTES FOR WOMEN" hung from the trees.

Mr. Lovelace made his way to the veranda of the Pavilion, where men sat on white porch chairs watching the activity and smoking cigars. Conrad ran off toward the roller coaster and the carousel.

As Mrs. Lovelace and Dorothy were greeted by several ladies, Mama and Emmie stood under a big shade tree. Mama explained to Emmie again what the suffragists, the people who were working to get the women's vote, were doing. Emmie had heard this explanation before, but Mama was so intent on its importance that Emmie knew she might hear it over and over in the coming months. The normally reserved Mama became so earnest when talking about suffrage.

"In Montana, men can vote for leaders like governors, senators, and the president and be involved in the government and the laws, but women can't vote at all. Wyoming women have the right to vote and now in Colorado, Idaho, and Utah too—nine states altogether. Now it's our time."

Mama was interrupted by Mrs. Lovelace bringing some friends over to meet her. When the ladies moved on, Mama kept at it, quietly but firmly holding Emmie's attention. "A vote is a very important thing to have.

When you vote, you have a say in what happens. It's a responsibility and an honor. Each vote makes a difference. If women win the right to vote, you'll be able to vote when you're old enough, and your daughters, and their daughters, and on and on. We will vote to force safety at the mines and many other important things." Emmie understood each word. Mama's hopes and now hers were riding on this issue.

When Mrs. Lovelace and Dorothy rejoined them, Mrs. Lovelace was breathless. "My, what a crowd," she exclaimed. "With rallies like this and the powers of Jeannette Rankin, I think we will get the vote!"

The rally began at eleven o'clock. Women, men, and children filled the grassy area to listen. Mr. Lovelace rejoined them. As the speeches rang out, the audience applauded and cheered. Jeannette Rankin was a slender, pretty young woman with a friendly smile, dark eyebrows, and intense eyes. She wore a yellow dress and a graceful, flowered hat covered her brown hair. A sash draped over her shoulder read "Votes for Women" in purple letters. When she stood to address the crowd, her voice was strong and confident. Her words were common-sense, clear, and direct. Emmie understood exactly what Miss Rankin meant when she said, "Men and women are like right and left hands; it doesn't make sense not to use both." Everyone clapped loud and long.

Mama put her arm around Emmie's shoulder. Emmie knew that Mama was shy and just starting to feel comfortable with lots of things about their new life, but she knew Mama was a strong person. If Mama could vote, things were bound to become more fair, she thought.

After the rally, the ladies spread out the food for the picnic. "Where is that Conrad?" Mama asked with exasperation.

"He's over by the roller coaster, Mama. He didn't even come to the rally," Emmie reported.

"It's okay," Dorothy chimed in. "Let's go get him."

"Hurry along, girls," Mr. Lovelace said. "We need to eat. It's almost time for the races to start."

Emmie and Dorothy found Conrad watching the roller coaster. "Come on!" Emmie said sternly. "You've almost missed the picnic."

Dorothy certainly didn't have a stern look on her face. "There's lots of food, Conrad," she said, sweet as syrup.

Emmie, Conrad, and Dorothy filled their plates high with fried chicken, potato salad, thick slices of bread with butter and jam, and deviled eggs sprinkled with red paprika and went to sit under a tree for their feast.

Conrad was munching on his fourth chicken leg when Mrs. Lovelace and Mama began to gather up the picnic dishes. He scurried over to snatch up a few cookies and handed an apple to Emmie. "Put this in your pocket for me, Em."

Mr. Lovelace stood up and said in an announcer's voice, "And they're off! Race time, folks."

# Chapter Four

## Bet on the Best Horse To Run Second

The atmosphere at the races was altogether different from the rally and picnic. Instead of lush green grass, flower gardens, and ladies in white dresses, this place was dusty and rowdy. Cowboys, horses, jockeys, and families were all jumbled into one crowd. Children climbed on the fences and grownups gathered in groups, laughing and talking. Horses reared up and pranced nervously as they were led around to the back of the track to corrals and stalls.

Emmie and Conrad had never been to a horse race before. Dorothy told them about it while her parents greeted everyone in sight. "Before post time—that's the start of the race—we get to look at the horses out back. It's a good chance to choose your favorites."

Mr. Lovelace chuckled at Dorothy's description. "We'll take a look at some of the ponies. I've got a few to put my money on today. There's a little horse I like here from Dillon. Boomerang. They call him Boomer. People say he'll run away with it. There's an old saying…" He gave the three children a steady look. "Bet on the best horse to run second. But never be second yourself."

It took Emmie a minute to figure out what Mr. Lovelace meant, but Conrad nodded like he knew right away. Sometimes, Emmie thought, Conrad tries to pretend like he knows everything. What was it about boys that made them not want to admit it when they didn't know something?

"Can we pet the horses?" Emmie inquired. Conrad gave her a look of sheer disgust.

"No," Mr. Lovelace said. "They get pretty excited before the race. Or we hope they do."

"We ladies will find a place in the grandstand," Mrs. Lovelace said. "You four go around back and we'll meet you for the first race."

Conrad strode along right beside Mr. Lovelace. Dorothy and Emmie stepped lively to keep up. A group of people gathered near a shiny black horse. The horse neighed and shook his head and the man holding him tightened the rope. "Boomer! Hey! Whoa! He's ready to run before the race even starts," the man said jovially.

Boomer was all shiny black except for a small white spot on his forehead and a little white above his hooves on his back legs. There were other horses to look at too. Chestnut browns, grays, big powerful horses, and smaller flighty ones. A man walked by and said, "First race. Ten minutes."

Mr. Lovelace and the other folks milling about started toward the grandstand. Dorothy, Emmie, and

Conrad lingered to take a last look. "We'll be there in a minute, Father," Dorothy said.

There was a long row of stalls with a horse in each one. Some of the horses seemed restless, but others stood quietly. At the far end of the row was Boomer's stall.

"Let's try to see Boomer up closer," Emmie said.

"You'd better be careful, Em. He's a high-strung racing horse." Conrad looked sternly at Emmie as if he knew all about racehorses. Dorothy just stood there, as if she knew all about Conrad.

"Maybe I can bring him luck," Emmie said.

"I don't know, Em," Conrad said. "We'd better get going." It was unlike Conrad to be cautious, but Emmie had noticed that ever since the fight episode, he seemed to think twice about most everything.

"Oh, come on," Emmie said as she walked toward Boomer's stall. The stall was a square enclosure with half-walls and a wood gate that held Boomer in. Half-way up it, a board went across that was just right to climb on to see clearly into the stall.

Conrad and Dorothy looked incredulously as Emmie climbed up on the board. The gate wiggled back and forth. It seemed rickety and Emmie almost fell off.

"Get down this minute, Emma Hynes!" Conrad sounded frighteningly firm.

"Ok, Ok." Emmie grinned at him. She'd gotten her chance to see Boomer up close and she was proud of herself. And he was beautiful with his long nose, his thick mane, and his strong legs. He was standing calmly. She hadn't bothered him at all.

The three of them turned to walk back down past the stalls to the grandstand. At the other end of the stalls, a man set down a bucket of oats and walked back toward the grandstand.

"You're crazy, Em. What if that man would have seen you climb up there?" Conrad said.

"Well, he didn't, so there. And Boomer has my good luck now," she retorted.

When they got almost to the end of the stalls, they heard a noise down by Boomer's stall. When they turned to look back, the gate to Boomer's stall had opened and he was ambling out!

"Oh, no!" they all gasped at once.

"I told you so, Em. You must have loosened the latch when you climbed up," Conrad said sternly.

Emmie could hardly believe her eyes. Boomer was out of the stall! How could they get him back in? What about the race? What about Mr. Lovelace? What about the man that left the oats? Had he seen them? What if people thought they'd opened the stall? What if Boomer ran away or got hurt?

"Connie!" she implored, reverting desperately to her old name for her brother, as if there was something he could do. But Conrad was frozen to the ground, unable to move. Dorothy stared at Boomer. The three of them stood there, speechless and horrified.

After what seemed like an eternity of shock, Emmie knew they had to do something, but Conrad and Dorothy looked paralyzed. "We've got to do something quick to get him back in," Emmie blurted. "You'll have to help me."

"How?" Conrad replied hopelessly. Just then Boomer walked a ways out into the dirt field right at the end of the stalls.

Emmie grabbed the bucket of oats. "C'mon. We can't move too fast or we'll spook him. Come on, Conrad, and I mean it!" She started down toward where Boomer stood. He had not moved too far from the stalls yet. Emmie walked first, Conrad second, and Dorothy tiptoed behind.

When they got closer to Boomer, Emmie said softly, "Dorothy, move far away from the stall. We'll walk real slow toward him, Conrad."

"It'll spook him, Em," Conrad grimmaced. "We're doomed."

"We've got to try," Emmie said resolutely. "Walk slow but steady."

When they got about halfway to Boomer, who was watching them warily, he gave them a quizzical look.

"Maybe we are spooking him," Emmie said. "Go back with Dorothy and both of you get out of Boomer's sight." She held out the bucket of oats and said softly, "Whoa, Boomer. Come here. Whoa." She let the sounds of the second "whoa" stretch out on the air.

"Whooooooaaaaaa."

Boomer turned his head to one side and looked at the bucket of oats.

Emmie's heart thumped. She knew time was running out. If they got any farther out in the field, Boomer might run. The race would start soon. "Here Boomer," she said pleadingly.

Boomer stood still and then started to walk toward her.

Emmie had never talked to a horse before, but the words just kept coming, as if she were talking to a person. He moved closer as she softly said. "Good boy, Boomer. Whoa. There, Boomer, there….Easy." She walked backwards.

Almost to the stall, Boomer pushed his head toward her and into the bucket. She pulled the bucket back, walked a few more steps, backing quickly into the stall. Miraculously, Boomer walked into the stall too. She put the bucket down. Boomer stuck his nose in the bucket. The bucket tipped over, spilling the oats.

Emmie made herself as skinny as possible and scooted along the wall while Boomer was occupied with the oats – and she was out the gate. She wished she could go back in to get the bucket, but she knew she couldn't. Someone would discover it, but she hoped they wouldn't know what happened or who did it.

Emmie latched the gate and checked it. Conrad and Dorothy reappeared out of the shadows. With Boomer safely in the stall, they collapsed in speechless relief. Emmie felt like a limp noodle, but eventually, she let out a little giggle.

Then Dorothy giggled too. "My lands!" she exclaimed, sounding just like her mother.

"We'd better get around to the races," Conrad said.

Emmie nodded and took a deep breath. On the way to the stands, she glanced back and whispered, "Good luck, Boomer."

As they neared the grandstand, they saw Mama and the Lovelaces sitting about halfway up.

Conrad stopped a minute and turned to the girls. "Well, we sure solved that problem. There's no reason to tell about the gate, you know."

"We know," they both said at once.

Emmie was so happy, she smiled to herself and whispered, "Let's bet on Boomer to run second. He might be kinda tired."

They slid into the seats their parents had saved for them. Boomer was in the third race. He looked sleek as he pranced onto the track. The jockey riding Boomer wore a bright yellow shirt. He reached down, patted Boomer, and whispered something in his ear.

The gun sounded a loud crack and the horses took off at the shot. As they rounded the first turn, Emmie lost sight of Boomer. The horses were all clumped together in a group and it was hard to see clearly over on the far side of the track. Emmie, Conrad, and Dorothy strained forward to watch.

As the pack came around the second turn, the horses spread out. Some lagged farther and farther behind and three surged forward, running nearly even with each other. Was one of them Boomer? Yes! Their eyes caught the flash of the jockey's yellow shirt and Boomer's shiny blackness amidst the flying hooves and dust.

The announcer's voice brought the horses home. "And it's Copper Canyon in front, Silver Pony second, and Boomerang in third. They're neck in neck. It's gonna be a close one, folks. But wait, here comes Boomerang on the outside. This one isn't over yet."

Emmie and Dorothy held hands, jumping up and down, yelling, "Go, Boomer, go!"

Boomer was running flat out. He was beautiful. His head was up, his mane flying, and his powerful legs carrying him forward. He thundered past the other horses and pounded to the finish.

"And it's Boomerang from Dillon by a length," the announcer shouted.

Emmie and Dorothy hugged each other. Mr. Lovelace reached out to shake Conrad's hand. "I'll make sure you three get to see Boomer up close after the races," he said.

"Yes, sir," Conrad gave the girls a sly grin. They'd all be glad to see Boomer up close – for the second time.

# Chapter Five

## Rain and Fire

Even with all the work to do at the boarding house, the summer days were long. In the evenings, the yards echoed with games of Kick the Can and Red Rover.

The boarding house and Philipsburg felt like home. From time to time, Mama went to Butte for meetings about the money from the mines. But sometimes, days passed by without clouds of worry coming into the sky.

By late July, it was hot and dry. At the boarding house dinner table, the conversation often centered on the lack of rain.

"Fields are turning brown already," said a man who had been staying with them for two weeks while he sold equipment to farmers.

"Forest looks like a tinderbox," muttered a young cowboy who lived with them on and off between jobs. "Sure hope my fishin' spots out on Rock Creek haven't dried up."

"You fellas just wait," Old Nels said, settling back and taking an after dinner puff on his pipe. "Them thunder clouds will turn to rain clouds."

Emmie used a special duster and pan to brush crumbs off the tablecloth so it wouldn't have to be washed until the end of the week. Each of the boarders had a cloth napkin in a ring that they used for several meals. Wash day was a day-long undertaking each week so the linens were used as long as possible.

The kitchen was so hot that she and Mama continually had to mop off their beet-red faces. But boarding houses that wanted to stay in business had better serve a meat and potatoes dinner every night, so in the hottest part of the afternoon, Mama and Emmie started up the stove and went to work. No matter the temperature, meat, potatoes, and gravy were on the dining room table at six every evening.

Emmie finished washing dishes and went out onto the back porch. The rough porch boards creaked as she sat down on the porch swing. The side-yard grass was dry and brown in places, but the hollyhocks beside the house stood bright and tall. Pink and purple sweet peas climbed up a trellis. The upstairs windows were open, with white curtains blowing out in the gentle evening breeze. Conrad had said there might be a neighborhood game of Red Rover so while she waited, Emmie swung back and forth. Sometimes after dinner, just sitting a spell felt good.

As dusk crept around the corner, Emmie felt so tired that she almost fell asleep right there on the porch swing. It was cooler now and getting dark. There were black clouds off to the west. She wouldn't mind if they didn't play Red Rover tonight. She went inside and up to her room tucked under the eaves in the attic of the boarding house.

Conrad's room was in the attic too, but he wasn't home yet from his evening rambles. Emmie loved the attic hideaway and she was happy to be up there by herself. She remembered that when they first moved in, she and Mama and Conrad all slept in the same room on the second floor at the end of the long hall of boarders' rooms. Even though it was the biggest of the bedrooms and had a little sitting area arranged at one end by Auntie Ruthie, with the three of them, it was still crowded. Emmie and Mama shared the double bed. That was a good thing because sleeping by Mama made Emmie feel safe.

There was hardly room to turn around with both Mama's and Emmie's clothes, the trunks they'd brought from Butte, and all of Conrad's stuff. Conrad's space was always a mess. His covers were all tangled up, and even if he made his bed, it still looked rumpled. He had a lot of junk: boards made into bull's eyes, a baseball bat, ropes, rocks, and a million other things. His clothes hung out from the drawers, even if he shut them.

From a door in the bedroom, a steep stairway led up to the attic. After a few months of being smashed together in one room, Mama had the idea of cleaning up a section of the attic to make bedrooms for Emmie and Conrad. Mama was good at having ideas, and once a thought came to her, she never let much time go by before she took action. After checking with Auntie Ruthie, she enlisted Old Nels and Tom Beam to help. They oiled the squeaky door, cleaned the stairs, shoved everything in the attic to one end, and opened the rusty window. They painted the attic walls and made a divider to separate the space into two areas. It was tiny, but Conrad and Emmie each had room for a narrow cot with soft sheets and blankets. Among the old pieces of furniture stashed in the attic, they found two small chests-of-drawers, one for each of them.

Emmie's bed fit in cozily right under the slanted ceiling made by the roof. Mama made curtains for the little window and found some old hooked rugs rolled in a corner and put them by the beds so Emmie and Conrad didn't have to put their toes right on the scratchy wood floor when they stepped out of bed.

As dusk turned to dark, Emmie snuggled down in bed with the sound of thunder way off in the distance and lightning flashing over the hills. Old Nels said to listen and count "Mississippi time" from when you see the first electric flash of the lightning until you hear its sharp reverberating crack, and that told how close the lightning strike was. One-Mississippi, two-Mississippi, three-Mississippi, four-Mississippi, five-Mississippi, crack! Each count meant the lightning was a mile away—far enough. Emmie heard Conrad on the stairs as she drifted off to sleep.

All of a sudden, she awoke to thunder that rattled and shook the house. She sat straight up in bed. It sounded like boards ripping apart. A blue white light flashed through the window. She counted. One-Mississippi-two-crack! It was quiet for only a second and then another thunderous rumble. There wasn't even a chance to count this one.

She jumped out of bed and ran down the stairs to Mama's bed. Another lightning bolt lit up the bedroom. Mama was awake too.

"Mama?" Emmie whispered.

"Get in bed here, Em." Emmie heard seriousness in her voice. She climbed in with Mama. In just a few minutes the town fire siren blared.

"Oh, no," Mama gasped as she got out of bed. The boarders' bedroom doors opened down the hall and Conrad appeared at the bottom of the attic stairs.

"You two stay here a minute." Mama's voice sounded worried. She quickly pulled on her clothes. In the middle of the night darkness, everything felt confused. There was a knock on the bedroom door.

Mama opened the door. In the dim light stood Nels, a serious look on his creased face, his white hair disheveled. "Good. You're up already. Conrad, Emmie, quickly get your clothes and shoes."

Conrad and Emmie flew pell mell up the attic stairs, grabbed shoes and clothes, and were back in Mama's room in an instant. They followed Nels down the stairs leading to the kitchen.

"Quickly, put on your clothes here in the kitchen. Stay on the porch." Nels said. "The lightning struck down at the Taylor place. There's fire and wind. The town has some men to fight it, but it's close to the woods. If the wind shifts, the fire could start this way. Keep a watch here. I'll be back when I can."

Three more of the boarders came around the corner of the house, running toward the fire.

The last building at the end of Broadway before the pine tree covered side of the mountain, one block from the boarding house, was the Taylor place with a two story house, a barn, and several sheds. The two Taylor girls were grown up and had moved away so Mr. and Mrs. Taylor lived alone. They had sold their horses, cows, and chickens and only had their big old yellow lab dog, Sandy, left. None of them were as young as they used to be, but they took care of each other. Mr. Taylor liked to talk to Nels. Mrs. Taylor was a kindly lady who often came to the boarding house to sit on the porch swing. She said it reminded her of the days when Ruthie lived there. They had been friends for a long time. The Taylors seemed like a Grandma and Grandpa.

Mama, Emmie, and Conrad stayed close to the boarding house, peering down the street and into the dark night, straining to get a glimpse of the fire. Orange and red flames licked the Taylor's shed. The smell of smoke wafted down the street as black plumes curled into the air. To their relief, they saw the old couple and their dog coming toward the porch.

Mama called out to them. Mrs. Taylor sat down, breathing heavily, and Mama patted her shoulder.

"Thank the Lord, it only struck the shed," she said after she caught her breath. "We heard it crack and saw the flames from the bedroom window. Albert got us out of the house so fast that I forgot my cane and glasses. I can't go back now though. The fire's too close to the barn and the house."

"Thank goodness you're all right. You'll be safe here for now," Mama said.

Emmie wished she hadn't said "for now."

"I'm going back," Mr. Taylor said, and even for an old gentleman, his steps were quick as he set off into the night. Their dog Sandy jumped off the porch and followed him.

Mrs. Taylor sat with Mama on the porch swing. Emmie perched on the step. Conrad paced in the yard trying to get a better view. He asked Mama if he could go down to the fire, but she said not now. He hovered near the porch, hoping she'd change her mind.

They all watched and listened. Every minute seemed forever as the sky grew more orange, and they saw bigger flames shooting up. If the flames spread to the barn or the house, the woods would be next. Or the wind might shift, sending the flames the other way, down the street into town, and towards them.

Except for the light from the fire and smoke, the sky over the valley was frighteningly black. The thunder continued to crash and lightning flashed through the sky. They huddled together on the porch, peering through the shadows. Again they heard the fire siren, calling any of the town's men who weren't already at the fire.

"Can't I go, Mama?" Conrad implored.

Mama looked at him seriously. "Ok, son. Be careful." He was off like a shot, running down the street to where the road curved into Taylor's place.

There was a big grassy area in front of the house and the other buildings were in the back near the creek with mountainside behind them. The shed was now a skeleton with flames illuminating it. Dark smoke billowed up. The fire gobbled its way toward the Taylor's vegetable garden by the barn.

Shouts of "over here" and "watch out" punctuated the crackling of flames and the whistle of wind as the men strained to get control over the fire's force. A line of men passed buckets of water hand over hand from the creek to the smoldering shed and the grassy area. When the water hit the coals and charred wood, it hissed, and more smoke arose. Conrad's eyes burned from the thick smoke in the air.

The firemen had a pump with a hose they put into the creek, but they had a problem getting the pump and hose to work. Desperate calls and instructions were shouted out while the flames grabbed at more and more of the grass, ever closer to the barn. The force and power of the fire turned the night to chaos.

Conrad ran to find Nels, Tom, and the others from the boarding house. They were digging a trench around the end of the garden to hold the fire there, but it wasn't working. The flames moved quickly and began to lick at the barn wall.

"Get a shovel and dig as fast as you can," Tom instructed Conrad.

Someone yelled, "Get that dog out of here!" Sandy ran wildly between the shed, the garden, and the barn, barking and searching.

Nels glanced to Conrad. "Can you get Sandy?"

"I'll try," Conrad replied. Sandy, totally agitated by the fire, wouldn't stop barking.

"Come on, Sandy. Here, girl." Conrad knelt down in hopes Sandy would come to him. She started toward him, then ran away.

"Sandy, Sandy!" Conrad yelled out into the mass of confusion. Sandy had disappeared into the darkness, but Conrad heard her barking.

"Grab that mutt!" a harried voice hollered.

Conrad called frantically for Sandy. All of a sudden, a desperate shout punctuated the night. "Stand back! Watch out!" Conrad heard a crashing thud, jumped back, tumbled over another person, and felt himself being pulled along the ground by his arm. A wall of smoke and flames leapt up as the side of the barn collapsed. Sparks flew into the sky like fireworks.

Conrad couldn't see Sandy anywhere or hear her barking. His eyes searched the smoky scene. He saw Nels and Albert through the smoke, but not Sandy. Plaintively, he yelled out, "Sandy! Come, girl."

"Out of the way!" yelled a man dragging the hose. Conrad heard a yip and there was Sandy. She limped over to Conrad on three legs and stood by him, whimpering.

"Sandy." Conrad knelt down and hugged the dog with relief. She sat down and licked her paw. She must have stepped on a hot coal. "We'll get you fixed up." Conrad took hold of Sandy's collar and coaxed her away from the fire. This time she walked along obediently, hobbling close to his leg. As they moved down the road, she eventually put down her paw and limped along on it.

When they got about halfway to the boarding house, there were Mama, Emmie, and Mrs. Taylor, leaning on Mama's arm. They had walked down the street to try to get a better view.

"Where's Albert? How's our house?" Mrs. Taylor's arm reached out to her dog, as her eyes searched Conrad's face.

"Everyone is fine," Conrad panted, "and the house so far, but the barn's on fire. Sandy can't be by the fire though. You hold her, Emmie. I gotta get back."

Emmie grabbed Sandy's collar to guide her toward the boarding house. She wished she could carry her, but Sandy was too heavy. Now walking on all four paws, Sandy strained to follow Conrad. It was all Emmie could do to hold her. When they got to the porch, Emmie struggled to get Sandy into the kitchen to keep her inside. Finally, once inside, Sandy lay down and licked at her paw. "You'll heal up, girl," Emmie soothed and quickly went back to the yard to watch.

The hose was now working so the men tried to beat back the barn fire with a steady stream of water. Just when the flames died down in one place, they leapt out in another. The men started a new trench between the barn and the house. Someone handed Conrad a shovel. He dug as fast as he could, his arms shaking with each shovelful.

"Bring the pump wagon over here!" a man shouted. Everyone ran to the other side of the barn.

"Let out more hose! Start the buckets too!"

Conrad dropped his shovel as he was given a bucket of water. He passed it on to the next person. The shed and garden were now left alone. This side of the barn was the last place to battle the fire before it reached the house. It seemed as though the fire was winning. Even all the men in Philipsburg were not enough to beat back the force of the flames.

As they desperately tried everything, Conrad felt a few drops of rain. At first he didn't notice it because he was working so hard. But, yes, it was rain. A few drops and then a few more fell on his head and shoulders.

Nels yelled, "Dear God, yes!" as the sky opened up and rain fell in sheets and buckets of cold, beautiful water. A cheer went up when they knew the fire would not get the house or the mountain. It wasn't totally out, but it was tamed.

Conrad stood between Nels and Mr. Taylor. They looked at the sky and let the rain pound on their faces.

Mr. Taylor put his arm around Conrad. "You saved Sandy, my boy."

"Yes indeed." Nels nodded, looking approvingly at Conrad. "Good man."

They monitored the fire for the rest of the night. As the grey dawn came, the rain stopped and the sky lightened with streaks through the clouds from the east over the broad Flint Creek Valley. The daylight showed what a fight they had fought. The shed and garden were totally gone. Black coals with puddles of rain water were all that was left. The barn was a charred skeleton of timbers. The smoldering piles of wood, grass, and hay smelled like old campfires. But the Taylor's white house, with moisture still on it from the rain, stood glistening in the dawn sun.

The fire fighters were beginning to disband when Emmie ran into the yard. Breathless, she called out to Nels and he hollered to the men, "Breakfast at the boarding house!"

# Chapter Six

## Auntie Ruthie

Mama and Emmie served mountains of pancakes to the exhausted fire crew. After everyone had eaten their fill and gone home, Emmie started to clean up, but Mama said something very un-Mama-like. "Let's leave this for later and take a little nap."

The boarding house was quiet in the middle of the morning. Conrad was already asleep up in the attic. Emmie lay down on the cool sheets beside Mama. A breeze from the open window blew the curtain. Emmie's eyes drifted shut.

"Is anybody home?" A woman's voice called up the stairs.

"Yes, we're here." Mama sat up from her nap. "I'll be right down."

Emmie heard the voices faintly, but couldn't get her eyes open. She fell back to sleep.

When she woke up, she wasn't even sure what time it was. Everything was quiet downstairs. The sun shining into the bedroom felt warm. She rubbed her eyes and remembered the fire, the night of fire fighting, and the breakfast. She lay there a few minutes reliving it all.

When Emmie got downstairs, Mama wasn't in the kitchen. She and Belle and Nels were sitting in the parlor. Emmie knew right away that something wasn't right.

"Come sit down, Emmie," Mama said seriously. "We have sad news."

Emmie slipped onto the settee beside Mama and Belle. They didn't look like themselves at all. Nels sat in the big armchair in the corner. He wasn't even smoking his pipe, which he always did when he sat in the armchair.

Mama spoke quietly. "It's Auntie Ruth. She died last night."

"Auntie Ruthie?" Emmie gasped. "Oh no, what happened?"

"She died in her sleep. We think her heart just quit working."

Emmie knew she should be brave for Mama and in front of Belle and Nels, but she couldn't keep from crying. Their Auntie Ruthie. Emmie remembered her standing in the front hall to greet them that first wintery day that they arrived at the boarding house. They were all so uncertain and afraid. The three of them stood there bundled in their coats and their hesitation. It had only taken one look at Ruthie greeting them with a welcoming smile to help them. She was a perfect "almost auntie"—a plump little lady with gray hair piled atop her head, glasses perched on her nose.

"Praise the Lord, you're here!" she had said in a voice

that sounded as friendly as her smile looked. She put out her hand to shake Mama's and said, "Oh pshaw," grabbed Mama, and gave her a big hug. To Emmie and Conrad, she said, "Hello, my dears. After such a long trip, you must need some cookies."

"I hate to leave this house, but I just can't keep up," Ruth repeated often during the days she spent showing them the details of running the boarding house. "I'll try to come see you as often as I can. A fine family like you will need an Auntie." This seemed to make her feel better about leaving.

That was how they began to call her Auntie Ruthie, instead of Miss Davies. She had become their honored auntie. Now she was gone.

Mama patted Emmie's hair. Nels took a bandana out of his pocket and wiped his eyes. Belle's pale blue eyes were filled with tears too. It was quiet in the room as they all sat there together.

Finally, Belle spoke, "She loved you all, you know."

Nels cleared his throat, but he didn't say a thing. He took his pipe in his hands.

Belle stayed at the boarding house for the next few days. They planned a funeral for Ruthie. Philipsburg had been her home for a long time. She would be buried in the cemetery where so many other Philipsburg pioneers marked the end of their days.

People came by the boarding house to bring food and flowers. It reminded Emmie of the days after Papa died, but she didn't want to be reminded of those days. Everyone who came to call had something nice to say about Ruthie. They told about the things she did to help everyone, the delicious food she shared, and the kind way she listened to everyone and made them feel special. Some people brought recipes she had given them.

Emmie's favorite thing in the kitchen was a set of red and white painted enamel pie plates with a rooster and a hen on them. On the hen pie plate it said, "May we love as long as we live." On the rooster one it said, "And live as long as we love."

Several people remarked on the plates. "That was Ruth, all right. Lots of love to give," one lady said. Even after Ruth's death, the boarding house was still welcoming people.

There was so much company for the next few days that dinnertime, which was always right on the dot of six, became later each night as Mama stopped to visit with people who came to call. Everyone at the boarding house pitched in to help. The cowboy pulled on an apron and peeled potatoes. A traveling salesman stirred the stew. A miner scrubbed his blackened hands until they glistened before he baked an apple pie.

Auntie Ruthie's funeral was held at the white church on the hill. Emmie had only been to one other funeral, and that was Papa's. That time she hadn't let herself cry because she knew she had to stay strong for Mama. This time, at least she knew what to expect. It was way too soon for another funeral, but somehow they had to do it.

On the day of the funeral, cars and buggies lined the streets. The church was filled to overflowing. Mama, Conrad, and Emmie sat in the front row with Belle, Nels, and the Taylors. Emmie was squeezed in at the very end on the aisle next to the high, dark wood end of the pew. Bouquets of flowers were on the altar and the steps leading up to it.

Before the service started, Emmie wanted to turn around to see the people filling the church, but she didn't know if she should look. She tried to catch a glimpse by turning her head slightly. She didn't quite understand funerals. Now she'd been to two of them. She knew it was supposed to help everyone. Maybe it did. But being so quiet and serious, it was hard to know if it did. Maybe it helped the grownups to have a time and place to cry. Instead of being like children who might burst out wailing any time or place, older people weren't supposed to cry unexpectedly. Even by eleven years old, crying was supposed to be pretty much controlled. But sometimes, Emmie did cry. She'd even thought that crying made a person feel better. So if it helped, how come you weren't supposed to do it? She guessed that was the reason for the funeral.

Emmie was concentrating hard on getting all these thoughts straight when the church organ hummed, and everyone stood to sing. Mama held the red prayer book and pointed to the places where there were psalms and prayers to say. The minister told some stories about Ruth. During that part, the service felt more relaxed. By the end, it seemed almost better, and there was more easiness filling the church.

During the last hymn, all the voices blended together, the men's deep booming, the ladies clear tones, and a few warbly high notes. Mama's bell-like voice, Conrad's emerging young man's voice, and Emmie's soft one chimed in on "Blest Be the Tie That Binds."

People's serious looks lightened as they filed out onto the church steps. Ladies held hands and hugged each other. Men shook hands. Emmie and Conrad were greeted by many of the people who told them how pleased Ruthie was that there were children living in the boarding house.

As they stood outside of the church, Emmie noticed Old Nels standing off by himself with his back to the crowd. He wore a dark suit, the nicest clothes Emmie had ever seen him in. The suit jacket was too tight. It looked like it might have been a jacket Nels brought from Sweden many years ago. Emmie walked over to him. When she saw his face and eyes, she knew he'd turned away from the others so no one would see him crying. He tried to fumble with his pipe, but his hands shook. His broad shoulders were hunched and bent. Emmie stood beside him quietly. He reached down and took her slim hand. They stayed there for a long time until Nels spoke softly, "Let's go home now."

That evening from her attic window, Emmie heard Mama, Belle, and Nels as they sat on the porch, talking in the twilight dusk.

"Such a tribute to her life. So many friends came today," Belle said wistfully.

"She would be pleased," Nels added.

Mama was very quiet. The sweet-smelling smoke from Nels's pipe drifted up into the attic window. Emmie heard Mama say, "I can't bear to think of leaving this boarding house." Mama said it so softly that Emmie wasn't sure she had heard it right. "With Ruth gone, the boarding house will be sold to a new owner."

"Don't think of it right now," Nels said quietly.

Leave the boarding house? Emmie bit her lip. She'd never had that thought before. Where would they go? What would happen? A new fear gripped her heart.

# Chapter Seven

## School Time

"I like your shoes, Emmie," Dorothy said as they walked to school on the first day of September.

Emmie looked proudly at her new shoes. "Thanks. Yours are pretty too."

Dorothy always had nice clothes, and Emmie was glad to have something new too. One reason Emmie liked Dorothy was that even though she had lots of clothes and pretty things, she didn't act like it was important. She always noticed even the littlest new or pretty thing someone else might have.

Dorothy had a peach colored bow in her hair to match her peach and green dress. She looked like something good enough to eat for dessert. She bounced along beside Emmie, carrying a canvas bag with new pencils, paper, and a lunch in a brown paper sack.

Emmie's hair was braided into her usual braids, and since it was first thing in the morning, not a single straggly hair had escaped yet. The braids were tied with red ribbons. With her green eyes and her bright smile, she too looked like a good dessert. Dorothy was peaches and cream; Emmie was apple cobbler with cinnamon.

Emmie's dress wasn't new. She only had a few dress-es, but this one was pressed and crisp, and it was her favorite. It had red embroidery on a white collar, with red and white gingham checked fabric. Her shoes were soft leather with white buttons going up the side. When she got them, Emmie told Mama she wished they could put the shoe money in the Boarding House fund instead.

"You are the best girl, my Emmie," Mama said. "But we can't have your toes poking out at the ends of your shoes! It would harm your feet to squeeze them into too small shoes. I think these new ones will last a long time. Anyway, we need a lot more than shoe money can buy."

As they walked along, Dorothy was breathless with news. "Our new teacher is Miss Mary Kathleen Moore. My Mama said she's nice—young and pretty too."

"We're lucky!" Emmie piped in. "You know who Conrad has? Mr. McBean."

"I know," Dorothy said, grimacing. "Good thing we're not in seventh. Mr. McBean should be able to make Danny Flaherty behave though. Except, poor Conrad. Don't you think, Em?"

Dorothy was becoming more than a little sweet on Conrad.

"He'll do fine, Dorothy. He's kind of smart. I'd never tell him that though." Emmie grinned.

"Maybe by the time we're in seventh, Mr. McBean will leave," Dorothy replied.

"Or… I will." A worried look crossed Emmie's face.

The past few weeks had mixed the anticipation of school starting with the sadness of Ruthie's death and worries about being able to stay at the boarding house. Dorothy didn't notice what Emmie said.

Before Ruth Davies died, she was making payments to the bank for the boarding house and employing Mama to run it. Now the bank would sell the boarding house to another owner. They would have to leave. Mama could buy the boarding house, but that seemed impossible.

Emmie knew that it was all tied up together: the boarding house, Auntie Ruthie's death, the bank payment, the money from the mining company, Papa's accident, their whole future. Even though Mama tried not to talk about it, Emmie noticed that she was quiet and worried these days. The bank had told her that she would have two months to raise the money for the down payment. Each day the clock moved steadily toward the deadline.

Thoughts and questions tumbled around in Emmie's head. How could they get the money? Would they have to move away from the boarding house? How would Mama earn a living? Would they be able to stay in Philipsburg? Would she be able to stay in school? What would Miss Moore be like?

When the playground was in sight, Dorothy nudged her in the side, and the activity overtook Emmie's worries. "Em, look over by the swings. No, wait! Don't look now. Oh well, they'll see us anyway."

Emmie's eyes focused on what Dorothy was sputtering about. There stood Monte and Bobby Montgomery, two brothers in fifth and sixth. They were the nicest boys in town and the cutest too. They hadn't been in Philipsburg all summer. Emmie was glad that they hadn't been there for the awful day of the fight. But even if they had been, Emmie was sure someone as nice as Monte Montgomery would never bet on a girl's fight. Emmie and Dorothy walked slower and slower as they took in the whole scene.

Conrad was right behind them. "Get a move on, you two," he said. "Hey, Mont," he called out.

For one grand moment, Emmie got a view of Monte Montgomery's smile. It was a grin to light up the world. She stood transfixed as he came over to them. She had no idea what she would say to him, but she hoped she'd get a chance to say something, anything. But, as soon as he got to them, Conrad took off. Monte followed him.

"Boys," she said to Dorothy and raised her eyebrows. She knew it was wasted on Dorothy though. She was far too gone on Conrad to come back to her senses now.

As they turned the corner of the school building, they stepped into the hubbub of opening day activity. There were first graders with their mothers, silly second and third graders acting goofy, stuck-up eighth graders, and, in front of the door, three teachers keeping the crowd at bay. Mrs. Featherly was the teacher for first, second, and third grades. She looked like a plump grandmother and that was good for the nervous first-timers. Mr. McBean, the teacher for seventh and eighth who was always mean and stern, was cheery and charming today because beside him stood the most amazing person Emmie had ever seen. A vision. Miss Mary Kathleen Moore.

Emmie and Dorothy fixed their eyes on this new teacher for fourth, fifth, and sixth. Their teacher. They looked at her in anticipation. She was not very tall, especially standing there next to the tall, skinny Mr. McBean and the solid Mrs. Featherly, but she had a straight way of standing and a hint of quiet confidence about her that made her seem just as tall and experienced as they were, even though she was young. She smiled eagerly and didn't seem one bit nervous that this was her first teaching day. She had dark brown hair and her eyes were clear blue.

The two girls stood there as if rooted to the spot. "Isn't she beautiful?" Dorothy whispered to Emmie.

Miss Moore wore a perfect teacher dress, navy blue with blousy sleeves, a delicate lace collar, and a long straight skirt to mid-calf. Her button-up leather shoes looked a bit like Emmie's.

Mr. McBean was so interested in Miss Moore that it took a long time for him to come to his senses and ring the school bell. When he finally rang it, children tumbled into the schoolyard from all directions. The teachers opened the doors. The crowd jostled forward.

The school was a two story red brick building. On

the first floor, Mrs. Featherly's first, second, and third grade room was on the left. Miss Moore's classroom for fourth, fifth, and sixth was across the hall. The seventh and eighth graders were upstairs with Mr. McBean. None of the younger children in their right mind would ever venture up there. This would be Conrad's first year on the second floor.

On the first floor a wide hallway with a wooden floor led to the stairs to the second floor at the far end. When all the children entered the hallway, it sounded like a last summer's thunder.

"No running!" growled a booming voice. Everyone stopped in their tracks. Mr. McBean had returned to his usual self.

Emmie and Dorothy stuck together and made their way to Miss Moore's room. Just as they were about to go in the door, Conrad and a group of boys passed by them. The words "Good Luck, Connie" popped out of Emmie's mouth before she even realized what she'd said. Thank goodness it was too noisy for him to hear her. But she meant it. This year would be different because she and Conrad were not in the same room.

Inside the classroom, Miss Moore had put up pictures on the walls and written on the chalkboard:

"Teachers open the door. You enter by yourself." (A Chinese Proverb)

That unusual writing must mean something, Emmie thought. It made her eager to know what. Maybe they were going to learn Chinese.

As the students came into the room, Miss Moore said, "Sit anywhere you like."

Sit anywhere you like? This was a switch. Last year there had been names taped to every desk, and that was where they had to sit.

Emmie and Dorothy found two seats in the middle row. Dorothy sat in front of Emmie, but then she stood up again and slid into the seat right beside her in the next row. "I won't have to turn around if I sit here," Dorothy said. "Remember last year? No turning around."

It took a few minutes for everyone to find a seat. They were busy looking at each other in disbelief because they could sit anywhere they wanted. Once that sunk in, it took a while to figure out where they actually did want to sit.

When everyone had found their seats, Miss Moore shut the door and walked to the front of the class. The children grew quiet, waiting to hear her speak. Just then, the door at the back opened again. There stood Clara. Miss Moore went back toward the door again, but she didn't look at all upset that someone was late.

"Good morning," she said, smiling at Clara. "There is one seat left for you." Clara didn't move. She stood in the doorway looking down. She didn't have a bag or any paper or pencils or anything. In her hands, she held a folded packet of newspapers wrapped around a square shape. That must be her sandwich, Emmie thought. Poor

Clara. She didn't even have a brown paper sack.

"Come with me." Miss Moore lightly touched Clara's arm to gently move her along. They walked together to the far side of the room where one desk remained empty. "Have a seat right here."

Miss Moore resumed the class. "Now we are all here," she said brightly. "Let the new year begin."

Miss Moore's voice was soft, but strong too. It was the kind of voice that made people want to listen.

"I am Miss Moore," she said. "I'm very glad to be here to learn with you."

Learn with us? A teacher learning too? Somehow this is connected to that Chinese saying, Emmie thought.

"We have so many things to do this morning," Miss Moore said, with her eyes scanning the room and touching on every student. "I want to tell you a story and to hear some of your ideas. We need to get to know each other and get arranged. This will be an important morning," she announced. "Let's start with who we are. How many of you are fourth graders? Please raise your hands."

Eight fourth grade hands hesitantly went up. Miss Moore counted and wrote the number eight on the board.

8

"Fifth graders, please raise your hands." Nine hands shot up eagerly. The fifth graders knew they were solidly in the middle. Plus, if their luck held, they might get to spend the next two years with this wonderful angel teacher. Miss Moore counted and wrote nine on the board in a column under the eight.

8
9

"Sixth graders?" She counted and wrote seven in the column.

8
9
7

"Now let's see. How many are we all together? Who can tell me?"

Emmie was still adding when she heard Miss Moore call on someone.

"It's twenty four," said an eager student.

"That's right." Miss Moore, added the numbers.

8
9
<u>7</u>
24

"But, wait," she paused. "There is one more person here."

A few eyes glanced at the late-arriving Clara, but no, she had raised her hand for sixth. Everyone looked puzzled. As the students looked quizzically at each other, Miss Moore smiled and turned to the board.

$$\begin{array}{r} 8 \\ 9 \\ \underline{7\phantom{0}} \end{array}$$
24 students
$\underline{+1}$ teacher
25 total in our class

"I'll be learning from you this year too," she said. "In fact, I already am."

The astonished students watched Miss Moore with eager eyes to see what surprise would be next.

"In a minute we will talk about this saying." She pointed to the Chinese proverb on the board. "I will tell you a story about a boy and a great Chinese teacher."

Emmie glanced at the clock. Twenty minutes had gone by. No one had said anything about Rules yet. There were starting to be lots of things Emmie liked. She liked the pictures on the walls. She liked Miss Moore's arithmetic on the board. She liked how Miss Moore had written plus one and added herself. She liked the writing on the board, even though she didn't know what a proverb was. She liked talking about learning. And she already loved Miss Mary Kathleen Moore.

"Now let's talk about seating," Miss Moore said. "For this first week, we will all mix together, seated alphabetically. That way I will get to know you, and you can get to know each other if you don't already. Whenever we are ready, we will decide together about how to put fourth, fifth, and sixth graders in groups."

Decide together? Neither Emmie nor anyone else could believe their ears. At that moment, all twenty-four children in the class would have gladly followed Miss Moore to the end of the earth.

"Here is a list of your names. As I call your name, please come to sit in the seat I am standing by. If you are already sitting in that seat, please get up and stand along the side of the room until your name is called. You may all gather your things to take them to your new seats. Does everyone understand?"

The students' heads bobbed in unison. Miss Moore moved over to stand by the desk in the front of the row nearest the windows. "A. Anderson, Byron," she said. A fourth grader popped out of his chair and went over to the desk. The girl sitting there picked up her things and moved over by the window.

This was going to be fun. Already Emmie wondered who she would sit by. Her mind raced, thinking of letters of last names.

"Miss Moore read the B's off the list and moved to the seat where Clara was sitting. Clara didn't look like she was about to get up so Miss Moore gently motioned her over by the windows. "Stand here for a moment, please," she said to Clara.

"Now D. Albert Clarence Day."

Some boys snickered.

"I go by Acey." The stocky sixth grader lumbered over to his desk.

"Thank you for telling me." Miss Moore made a correction on her list and moved on to F. "Flaherty, Clara." Clara took the last seat in Row One.

Emmie got so caught up in watching the moving that she forgot to notice that the letters were moving closer to H.

"More F's. Flint, Douglas. Right here." Miss Moore continued on as children shuffled in and out of the seats. "In this place, Jack Flint." Everybody liked the Flint brothers, fourth and fifth graders that told such good jokes they could make a dog laugh. It would be fun to sit by them, Emmie thought. The Flints raced each other to their seats and plunked down.

Miss Moore was now standing in the middle of the second row. "H. Hynes, Emma."

Emmie was already sitting right across from her new seat. She hesitated a minute and didn't know if she should say anything about her name, but Dorothy looked at her. This gave her courage.

"People call me Emmie, Miss," she said.

"I like that name," Miss Moore replied. Emmie was glad she'd spoken up. She scooted over, right behind the Flints. A good seat, she thought, but now, surely Dorothy wouldn't be near.

Miss Moore continued on. Even with the re-shuffling and exchanging, the group stayed quite orderly. When it got a little noisy, Miss Moore said, "Let's stay to our purpose, class," and miraculously, everyone did. That this teacher, who wasn't even very tall, could keep so many children orderly when exchanging seats was quite amazing. The seating moved through a J and a K.

"L. Dorothy Lovelace," Miss Moore next called out. Emmie's and Dorothy's eyes met excitedly, knowing they would be so near to each other.

Miss Moore was now standing right beside Emmie at the desk across the row from her as she called out, "M. Montgomery, George Montcalm."

What luck! Emmie rejoiced. Dorothy one seat away and Monte Montgomery right beside her.

"Just Monte is fine, Ma'am," George Montcalm Montgomery said with that smile again. Emmie and Dorothy tried hard not to look at each other to avoid dissolving in giggles.

"Robert Montgomery right here," she said, moving on down the row. "Is that Bobby?" She was getting the point of the nicknames.

There were still a few children standing by the sides,

but the seating moved along more quickly until the last person took his seat, a U, Nicholas Underwood. There weren't any Z's.

"That's it." Miss Moore moved to the front of the room. "Let's give ourselves a hand." She began clapping.

Everyone clapped and eased into their newfound places. What an hour already! Numbers, letters, moving, clapping. The time was flying by.

"Now that we are all settled," Miss Moore said, after the clapping had stopped, "I would like you to do a bit of writing. Please take out paper and a pencil. We are going to write about our hopes for this year."

Emmie was looking in her school bag when she heard someone whisper, "Hey, Emmie." It was Monte across the way.

"Got a pencil?" he grinned sheepishly.

"Um. Sure." Emmie quickly dug into her bag, praying that she'd find an extra pencil. She reached across and handed him her best pencil. Hopes for this year? Oh, yes, Emmie thought. She had nothing but hopes for this year. Right beside the hopes sat a heap of worries.

# Chapter Eight

## The Fair

Mama went to Butte twice during the first two weeks of school. After the second time, she came home so discouraged that she said, "I don't think the mine owners will ever turn loose of that money." Mama seldom seemed angry, but that night she did. So much was riding on that money.

The next night after dinner, Emmie and Conrad were surprised when she said, "We need to talk about going to the fair."

The Fair! Emmie's heart soared as they sat down in the parlor. Since before school even started, people had been talking about the Montana State Fair at the end of September in Helena, the state capitol. Emmie heard Miss Moore talking to Mrs. Featherly about going to a suffrage parade that would be held during the fair. But with their troubles, Emmie hadn't had a prayer of being able to go.

"The Lovelaces have invited us to go to the fair and the parade with them," Mama said. "We will drive to Anaconda and take a special train from there to Helena. We've been invited to stay with the Lovelaces' friends in

Helena. The Montgomery family is going too, so if you like, Conrad, you can ride with them."

"Will we all fit in their car?" Conrad asked.

Emmie thought, oh, hush up! To go anywhere with the Montgomery family, she'd be willing to sit on the roof if necessary. She couldn't believe her ears. Quickly, she tried to come down to earth and dim her beaming smile. If Conrad finds out about my liking Monte, he might tell him. That would be too embarrassing. Cringing at the thought, she tried to listen to Mama's details.

Mama had to make a lot of plans to be away for three days. "We'll make the meals ahead of time for the boarders, and Mrs. Taylor will come to serve them. It will only take a little bit of money. It will be worth it. This is our chance to stand up for suffrage. We can't miss it," she said with determination.

The next week flew by with planning. At school, Miss Moore said that there was to be no talking about the fair in class because not everyone was able to go. Emmie and Dorothy understood why, but on the walk home each day they planned and anticipated every detail.

On the day they were to leave for the fair, two cars drove up in front of the boarding house before sunup. Mama and Emmie got into the Lovelaces' car. Conrad hopped in with the Montgomery family and squeezed into the back seat with Monte and Bobby. Mr. Montgomery was a big, friendly man with a deep laugh. Mrs. Montgomery was a beautiful dark-haired lady wearing a

straw hat trimmed with a yellow ribbon. Everyone wore
sweaters and coats in the early morning dawn chill.

"Who arranged these passenger lists?" Mr. Montgomery called to Mr. Lovelace. "You have a car full of
pretty gals, and I've got three wild boys."

"Just plain luck," Mr. Lovelace yelled as he moved
to the front of the car and turned the crank to start the
engine.

After a few turns and a sputtering noise, the car
motor revved up. Mr. Lovelace slid into his seat behind
the steering wheel, and they went humming down the
road. The sun came up over the mountains, warming the
air, and glinting on the autumn yellow aspen trees. The
leather seats of the car smelled good. Emmie wished they
could keep driving forever, enclosed in the car's happy
cocoon with the Montgomery's car in sight up ahead.

By nine a.m. they pulled up to the train station in
Anaconda, took their bags out of the cars, and hustled to
the platform filled with excited people, all anticipating
boarding the shiny train bound for Helena and the Fair.
The engine car was decked out with the United States
flag and the flag of the State of Montana. The Montana
flag had a picture of the sun shining over the mountains
and the Great Falls of the blue Missouri River. Below
were the words "Oro y Plata," for gold and silver.

As the people talked and jostled about, a loud train
whistle blew several times. Steam hissed out of the engine in a puff. "All aboard for the Fair," a conductor

boomed in a loud voice. Everyone clambered on board to find their seats.

"Can we sit wherever we like?" Conrad asked Mama, as the crowd carried them along.

"Stay in this car," she replied, struggling to put her bag on the rack above the seats.

"I'll get it, Mama," Conrad volunteered and hoisted the bag up above his head onto the rack.

As the adults found seats, Emmie and Dorothy spotted an empty space on the right side near the end of the train car. The girls slipped past the people arranging themselves and plopped down into the empty place. The seat facing them was vacant until the three boys, Conrad, Monte, and Bobby sat down.

"All aboard, gals," Monte laughed, as he nabbed the seat by the window. Emmie was by the window too. Their knees were almost touching.

With a few more loud train whistle blasts, they were off, the train lurching, then clickety-clacking down the track. Emmie and Dorothy played Tic-Tac-Toe and Hangman as the trees and hillsides flew by outside the window. The boys occupied themselves with roughhousing until Mr. Montgomery came up and stopped them. Then they played Rock, Paper, Scissors, which gave them a chance to still swat at each other good-naturedly without getting into trouble.

"When we get to the Fair, let's go on the Ferris wheel," Monte suggested.

"Let's do," Emmie replied eagerly. Then she noticed Conrad's disapproval of her quick response. Maybe Monte was just talking about the boys. She wasn't quite sure what a Ferris wheel was, but she figured she'd take a chance on almost any kind of wheel if it had something to do with Monte Montgomery.

When the train pulled into Helena, the whistle blasted, and the steam from the train made a loud hissing noise. People were jolted back and forth as the train jerked to its final shutdown. The passengers stood up to gather their bags.

They stepped off the train onto a platform crowded with people making their way to the front of the station. Automobile horns squawked. "Come along now, children," Mrs. Lovelace directed as they made their way to their friends' shiny black automobiles. They all piled into the cars for the drive through the main streets of Helena.

As they drove along, Mr. Lovelace explained that the downtown part of Helena was called Last Chance Gulch because in the early days the miners had taken one last chance to find gold there. Helena was a bustling, busy, capitol city, filled with people from all over the state of Montana. Emmie thought that for them though, it should be called First Chance Gulch. It was the first chance to see what fun they were going to have.

Sandwiched in between Dorothy and Mama and a big suitcase, she managed to peek out the window.

Helena reminded her of Butte, but the narrow streets here twisted and curved through the downtown. The car moved slowly through the traffic until they came to a beautiful neighborhood with tree-lined streets and big houses.

They pulled into the driveway of a grand red brick house and were greeted by their host and hostess, Mr. and Mrs. Flute. The girls and Mama were shown to an upstairs bedroom. The delighted boys discovered that they would sleep in a tent in the back yard. It was late afternoon by the time they settled in, but there was still time to go to the fair.

The fairground was a small city in itself with a rodeo arena and grandstand, green tree-shaded lawns for picnics, and exhibit buildings to show off everything from cows, chickens, and pigs to pies, jams, and quilts. Beyond all that, a carnival glittered in a dusty field. A merrily spinning carousel, booths to win prizes, and a tall wheel-like contraption with bucket seats attached to it beckoned them. That must be the Ferris Wheel, Emmie thought. It looked at least ten stories tall.

Mr. Lovelace told the children that they would meet back at the entrance in two hours. "Don't get lost," he warned them. The boys headed straight towards the Ferris Wheel and Dorothy and Emmie hurried to keep up.

As they walked up to it, the tall, gigantic wheel circling around and around loomed overhead. Emmie gulped. All the people riding in the seats that swung from it waved happily to their friends below. At least it was a good sign that they were still smiling, she tried to reassure herself.

One man sold tickets. Another worked with the steam engine that turned the wheel and the lever that made it go back and forth and stop and go. The boys, Emmie, and Dorothy got in line. When they got to the ticket man, he took their money and motioned them onto a wooden platform.

The Ferris wheel creaked to a slow stop as each bucket seat came down to the platform. When the lever man pulled the big lever down to stop the wheel, two people got out of the slightly swinging seat, and two more got in. The wheel cranked around to the next two passengers, until all the passengers were exchanged, and all the seats were filled with new riders ready for a spin.

When their turn came to get on, the man motioned to them to hurry up to the seat. There was no turning back. He pointed to Emmie first so she hurried over to the seat and sat down on the sticky black leather, expecting Dorothy to be beside her. But Dorothy lollygagged behind, trying to engineer a way to sit with Conrad.

"Hurry up, you kids," the man said gruffly as he held onto the seat which swung back and forth over the platform. For a minute, Emmie thought, oh no, I'll have to ride all by myself.

The man motioned to the others. "You, son, come on!" he said sternly. All of a sudden, Monte slid in beside her, and the ticket man latched a steel bar over their laps. The ticket man swung the seat slightly. They rose off the platform and up into the air. Emmie's feet swung beneath her. She looked up. It was a long way to the top. She couldn't look down.

"This is swell," Monte exclaimed.

"Yes," she squeaked. Here she was, the wonderful Monte right beside her, but her heart pounded, and her stomach churned. What if I throw up?

The wheel kept stopping and going as new pairs of riders got on. It took a long time for Emmie and Monte to get to the top of the wheel. It seemed about fifty feet up in the air. Emmie grasped the bar and tried to focus up to the blue sky. Finally her eyes glanced out over the whole scene. It helped to look out, instead of down.

The fairgrounds with all the people, cars, horses, buggies, and sheds looked like a little play village. Off in the distance the mountains were blue and hazy. From up there, the mountain called The Sleeping Giant looked even more like a snoozing giant with a big rock nose. The sounds of the carousel music drifted up to their ears. Her hands weren't gripping the bar quite so tightly now. Maybe, she thought, she could manage to get one hand free to smooth her skirt if it flew up. The seat swung as the last riders got into their seat below.

The wheel started to turn faster. There were delighted squeals from the riders, but Emmie didn't let out a peep. The lever man way below had the lever pushed all the way forward. They plummeted down one side, flew over the wooden platform, past the lever man, and up to the top again. It was like spinning around on a giant, fast-moving clock.

Emmie's braids blew straight out in the wind. Once she got used to it, flying around and around was sort of breathtakingly fun.

Monte yelled to Conrad and Dorothy one seat below them. "Hey, down there!"

"Hey, up there!" Conrad yelled back and waved.

Emmie didn't let go of the bar though. She just raised up one finger from her firm hold on the bar and wiggled it at Dorothy.

Just when Emmie started to relax and really enjoy it, the end of the ride came quickly. It didn't seem nearly long enough when the man pulled the lever forward. The chairs stopped one by one to let the riders out. When Emmie first stood on solid ground again, her legs felt like rubber. Taking the steps down off the platform, Dorothy looked like a spindly-legged colt, learning to walk all over again.

Conrad made his legs go even more wobbly than necessary and walked wavy and silly. "Some ride!"

"Sure was," Monte agreed. The boys took off toward the automobile exhibit shed. Emmie and Dorothy headed to the suffrage booth to tell their mothers of their adventure.

It was easy to find the booth decorated with Votes

for Women banners. Mrs. Lovelace and Mama were there with other ladies. Pitchers of lemonade and cookies sat on a table for passers-by. The mothers listened as the girls described their Ferris wheel adventure.

"Come ride on it with us tomorrow, do, do. At first it's scary, but then it's fun," Emmie exclaimed breathlessly.

"You were brave to try it," Mama answered.

"My lands, yes," Mrs. Lovelace added.

That night, Emmie's eyes closed almost the minute her head lay down on the soft pillow in the Flute's upstairs bedroom. As she fell asleep, she thought of the wonders of the day and what the next one might bring.

# Chapter Nine

## A Parade for the Vote

Mama gently tapped Emmie's shoulder. "Rise and shine. Today is our suffrage day."

Sun shone through the window. Emmie never slept this late. At home, she was always up before dawn to help with breakfast. Now here she was in Helena, in a four poster guest bed, in a house bigger than any house she'd ever been in. The sun glittered off the copper dome of the Montana state capitol building on the hill and filtered in through lace curtains. She hopped out of bed.

"Dorothy, wake up," she said. "It's suffrage day."

Dorothy sleepily opened one eye and flopped over.

Emmie carefully took their dresses out of the tall polished wooden armoire. Emmie's dress was her yellow pinafore again. She didn't have that many dresses. Dorothy had a new white dress with a yellow waistband.

Dorothy yawned a little grumpily. Emmie knew from other times that Dorothy was not a very quick waker-upper. "It won't be easy to keep these dresses clean at the fair, you know, Em," she grumbled.

"But, Dorth, we have to," Emmie replied seriously. "For the parade later. That's the biggest thing."

"Come along you two," Mama intervened. "Here, Em, let me braid your hair."

As Dorothy inched out of bed and slowly pulled on her clothes, Mama worked to gather Emmie's hair into one thick braid. When they were dressed and ready, Mama took a glance in the mirror at her own yellow blouse and black skirt.

As they went down the curved staircase to the dining room, they could smell the scent of breakfast. Mrs. Lovelace and Mrs. Flute brought out steaming platters of eggs, sausages, and pancakes.

"Please sit here, Mrs. Hynes." Mrs. Flute motioned to Mama who was standing by the table. "And you two girls right here."

Emmie sat between Mama and Dorothy. It felt so funny to Emmie to be served breakfast. Usually she served the food to the boarders. She caught Mama's eye and knew Mama was thinking the very same thing.

"This is lovely," Mama said shyly to Mrs. Flute.

"I am glad you are here," Mrs. Flute said kindly. "And you too, Emmie dear. Thank goodness all the men went out to the fair early. Now we can take our sweet time. I'll drive us out to the fair grounds. Woman at the wheel!"

When they were finished eating, Emmie and Dorothy looked at the signs for the parade stacked by the door.

"I like this one. I can't wait to be a voter," Emmie said. The sign read:

## VOTING RIGHTS FOR WOMEN
## FUTURE VOTER.

"These signs are kind of big," Dorothy said. "How far are we walking anyway?"

"As far as it takes to get to the ballot box," Em replied, standing up tall as if she was giving a speech. "Do I sound like Miss Rankin?"

"Exactly. Emma Rankin." When Dorothy grinned, Emmie was glad she was finally wide awake and ready to go for the day.

Dorothy dug through the signs. "Here's one for the boys to use," she said, holding up a banner attached to a carrying pole with the words,

## I WANT MY MOTHER TO VOTE.

"I think Conrad does want Mama to vote," Emmie said seriously. "Voting on keeping our boarding house, for sure."

"I'm certain he would," Dorothy said dreamily.

"You would like Conrad if he wanted a pig to vote." Emmie poked Dorothy with the end of the pole.

"Only if a woman pig could vote," Dorothy replied, and they both giggled.

The car bounced along on the road to the fairgrounds. Mrs. Flute was not a timid driver. The canvas top of the

Flute's car was folded down so the ladies held onto their hats. As they got close to the Fairgrounds, they could hear the din of activity.

They parked near the stock barns. "Phew!" Dorothy said, holding her nose. "Good thing the booth is on the other side of the grounds."

Near the Suffrage booth, Emmie and Dorothy spotted their teacher, Miss Mary Kathleen Moore. She made her way through the crowd over to them.

"Hello, you two. Isn't this just grand?" she said as she put an arm around each of them. "I'm so glad you could come, Mrs. Hynes," she said, shaking Mama's hand.

When the mothers gave permission for the girls to look around the fair, the two friends took off in a flash. First they saw a five and a half pound potato that had won a potato contest, and next, an automatic cow-milking machine with a life-sized glass cow to demonstrate the process. They were leaving the cow-milking machine when whoops and cheers from the rodeo grandstand beckoned them to a show of daring cowgirls from the Irwin Wild West Show doing riding tricks.

They climbed up into the grandstand and watched while the cowgirls, with their silver belts flashing and their hair flying, stood up on the backs of their horses and rode full speed across the arena. Just as it looked as though they would crash into the fence, dust flew up, they reined their horses up tight, screeched to a stop, and waved their cowboy hats at the crowd. Everyone whistled and cheered. Now those are brave girls, Emmie thought. I bet a Ferris wheel wouldn't faze them.

After they left the grandstand, Emmie and Dorothy decided to treat themselves to apples on a stick dipped in smooth, brown, creamy caramel. They held the sticks out in front of themselves and craned their necks to eat carefully without dripping any of the gooey sauce on their dresses.

By late in the afternoon, it was time to go to downtown Helena for the Suffrage Parade on Main Street. At the place where the route started, there were bands, floats, cars, horses, wagons, and people in all sorts of costumes, even someone dressed as Sacagawea, the Shoshone woman who guided Lewis and Clark. As everyone got into position for the procession along the crowd-lined main street, ladies, children, and men all milled about greeting one another enthusiastically. Mrs. Lovelace gleefully announced that six hundred people from all over Montana were here to march for suffrage.

The jostling crowd filled the street, the sidewalks, and even stretched down the side streets. Emmie and Dorothy stayed near their mothers, Conrad, and the Montgomery boys in the crush of people.

The crowd parted to allow a group of distinguished looking people to make their way through. There were several tall men in dark suits and ladies with long skirts, jackets, and fancy hats who stopped for handshakes and greetings with the people in the crowd. One of the ladies was Jeannette Rankin, the same famous leader of the movement to give women the vote in Montana that they had heard speak in Butte.

The group stopped right by them. "Here's our Philipsburg contingent," one of the gentlemen said. "Allow me to introduce Mrs. Julia Lovelace and her daughter Dorothy and...," he paused to allow Mrs. Lovelace to introduce those he didn't know.

"My friend and neighbor, Mrs. Honora Hynes and her daughter, Emmie," Mrs. Lovelace filled in graciously. "The young men are Conrad Hynes and George and Robert Montgomery."

Up close, in her gold velvet suit and with her intense brown eyes, Jeannette Rankin was even more memorable. She greeted them as if they were the most important people in the whole world. Everyone shook hands politely. When meeting Mama, Miss Rankin grasped Mama's hand in both of hers. "I think I know of you, Mrs. Hynes. Aren't you the person who is seeking to receive a settlement for your husband's death from the mining company?"

"Yes, I am," Mama nodded.

"My brother, Wellington, knows Will George, the Butte lawyer working on this case," Miss Rankin said. "He's told us of you and your children. I'm so sorry about your husband. I admire your courage. The mines must be made to pay these benefits. We all have a fight before us. Do stay strong. I hope we'll meet again." Then, in one second, she disappeared into the crowd.

Mama, Emmie, Dorothy, and Mrs. Lovelace stood in delighted awe, blinking at Miss Rankin's presence and her recognition of Mama.

"My, my," Mrs. Lovelace exclaimed. "Here we go!" she said excitedly as the crowd began slowly moving down the wide street.

Mama took Emmie's hand and squeezed it as they walked in the long line of suffrage marchers. A band played up ahead and people chanted, "Votes for Women Now," as they waved their signs. From the sidelines, some people clapped to show support, but others stood glumly watching them pass by. One man held up a sign that said:

### WOMEN BELONG IN THE HOME
### NOT AT THE BALLOT BOX.

Emmie smiled at him, but he didn't smile back. She wished she could stop to tell him that women belonged in both places. Men were in two places, working and at the ballot box. Women should be too. How could anyone not want women to vote?

Conrad, Monte, and Bobby took turns carrying their banner, one on each end of the pole.

"Look up there." Conrad pointed to a several story grey brick building. Some women leaned out a window on the second story holding a long VOTES FOR

WOMEN sign. As the marchers passed by, they waved up at the ladies in the window.

At one point, the parade came to a stop when a two-seater automobile got too close to some riders on horseback. The startled horses reared and snorted. Mama pulled Emmie to the side, ready to jump out of the way if need be. Finally, with the help of some onlookers, the riders calmed the horses, and the parade started up again. The marchers stopped and started over and over as the wild colorful line made its way toward the Auditorium where the rally and speeches would be held.

The building didn't look big enough to hold this surging crowd. People squeezed through the double doors and flocked into the big room. The stage was decorated with flags and banners. A huge American flag hung from the ceiling. Attached to it were the names of the states that already allowed women to vote. Behind the speakers' podium stood bright yellow flags for each state that was working to get the vote like Montana. The group from Philipsburg found a place about halfway back in the crowd facing the platform.

The speakers on the stage were the same group of people who had worked their way through the crowd. Emmie hoped Jeannette Rankin would speak, and she did. As her strong voice carried over the crowd, Emmie thought, she shook my hand.

Emmie listened proudly as Jeannette Rankin said, "Do you know that the woman who rises at 6 to cook breakfast, who gets the head of the house off to work, and then takes care of the baby, dresses and feeds the children and sends them to school; the woman who scrubs and cooks and irons and bakes and sweeps and mends until she has to cook dinner and get ready to entertain her husband all evening, is listed in the census as without occupation? The woman who works in the home is as much of a worker as any other and needs the same representation in government."

Mama is doing this, and she's all alone, Emmie thought. She wasn't sure what the census was, but she knew that an occupation was a job and that Mama had a big one. Emmie remembered the grumpy man's sign during the parade. Miss Rankin said that women needed to be working at home with their families—and voting. These ideas described Mama exactly. Without Papa, Mama's vote was even more important. It gave their family a say in the world.

The crowd clapped wildly. Miss Rankin gracefully put up her hand to motion them to silence and continued, "You know that when you are working a problem in mathematics, you must take account of every factor if you are to get the right answer. So it is with government. Unless you take account of every factor, the answer will always be wrong."

These words were clear for everyone from ten to one hundred ten to understand. The sound of clapping filled the room as the crowd interrupted the speech over and over. Emmie's hands stung from clapping.

When she concluded her speech, Miss Rankin looked at the crowd with a determination that seemed capable of carrying these Montanans all the way to Washington, D.C. The cheering rose to the rafters.

After a long applause, a tall man introduced the next speaker, the President of the National Woman Suffrage Association. Her name was Dr. Anna Howard Shaw. She was a very small woman, but when she spoke, her words rang out and she seemed to grow taller. The huge crowd listened in attentive silence. Imagine, a woman who was a Doctor. Emmie's mind soared.

The rally lasted long into the September evening. It was chilly as they headed back to the big brick house. Emmie walked along on one side of Mama with Conrad on the other.

Conrad spoke first. "Thank you, Mama. It was a great day. I sure hope you get to vote."

"Me too," said Emmie.

Mama looked up at the moon and the stars glittering in the Montana night sky.

When at last Emmie, Dorothy, and Mama snuggled into their beds, the two girls whispered about all the events of the past two days.

"That Monte Montgomery's sweet on you, Em," Dorothy said.

"You should talk," Emmie replied. "You and my own brother."

For a minute they forgot that Mama was in the room, but it didn't matter. Mama was a girl too, just a grown-up one. She didn't tell them to quiet down. Their soft voices grew sleepier and sleepier until it was quiet. The only sound was the gentle breathing of sleep.

# Chapter Ten

## Halloween Snow

After coming home from the Fair, Emmie hoped every day that the cloud of uncertainty about the boarding house would blow away with the autumn winds. It didn't.

Mama was often sitting at her desk adding and re-adding the ledger book when Emmie got home from school. Mama was quiet and worried these days, but she always tried to cover it up and ask about Emmie's day.

Conrad didn't walk home right after school because he stayed to play football. When he did get home, sometimes he had some bruises, but he was always grinning ear to ear. Usually he started right in on the late afternoon chores of filling the wood box, but some days, he opened the door and let out a whoop. "Touchdown, Ma, Conrad Hynes Touchdown!"

"Great, son. Your Papa would be so proud."

During the autumn days, their troubles piled up like crackling leaves. One night in late October when Mama asked Emmie and Conrad to sit with her in the parlor, Emmie knew it would be bad news.

"I have a heavy heart to tell you this," Mama said, "but we are a family and we share everything. I have something hard to tell you. I don't think we can stay here at the boarding house too much longer."

It shouldn't have been a surprise to Emmie. Even though she hadn't wanted to think about it, there weren't as many boarders as there had been during the busy summer. Mama looked more and more worried every time she worked at her desk.

Emmie and Conrad sat in stunned silence. Finally Conrad said, "Isn't there any way to stay, Mama? I like it here now. We have our friends...school...football."

"I know," Mama said sympathetically. "Since Auntie Ruthie died, I've been trying to save money so we could buy the boarding house, but the bank's deadline for me to come up with a down payment is nearly over. I just don't have the money."

"What will the bank do?" Emmie asked.

"They will put the house up for sale and a new owner will be found." Mama gulped. "We'll have to move back to Butte. We will have a place to live there and I can find work."

There it was. Not just "we'll see what happens" or "we'll think of something," but rock solid, right out on the table—moving back to Butte.

"Where will we live?" Emmie asked desperately.

"We can live with Aunt Louise and Uncle Henry until I find work so we can get a place of our own."

"Uncle Henry?" Conrad muttered.

"He's mean," Emmie gasped, speaking the awful truth.

"We'll only stay with them as long as we have to. I promise you I'll try to get us our own place as soon as I can. I'm so sorry. I know you're both happy here."

Then Mama lost hold of her bravery and cried. Emmie hugged her from one side and Conrad from the other.

"I miss your Papa," she said softly, almost as if saying it might bring him back.

"Me too," Emmie whispered.

Conrad put his head in his hands. "Me too."

For a long time, they just sat there. Discouragement and sorrow overcame them. They didn't often let it in the door, but tonight, it filled the parlor.

Conrad broke the silence. "I'll go to work," he said. "Boys can start at the mines when they're fourteen."

"No, Conrad," Mama said resolutely. "You'll get your education. You'll never work in the mines, never underground."

A tight knot of worry gripped Emmie's stomach. Usually she put on a cheerful face, and she had gotten so good at it that it came on automatically, and no one knew about her worries. But not this time. She couldn't do the only thing that would set their ship afloat again —save the boarding house.

"I was hoping Mr. George, the lawyer from Butte,

would have some success with the settlement for the miners' families," Mama said, "but so far there is nothing. I've tried everything to find a way."

If there was a way, Emmie knew Mama would find it. Their quiet, strong, gentle Mama. Their Mama who had somehow gotten them to this boarding house. Their Mama who wasn't afraid to go up against a huge mining company to fight for what they deserved in Papa's honor. Their Mama who had finally begun to smile here in Philipsburg's hopeful shelter.

How could things be so bad and so good all at the same time, Emmie wondered, as she laid in her attic bed that night. School was great. Miss Moore was the world's best teacher. Each day was fun. Since the first day's loaning of the pencil, Monte Montgomery had borrowed tons of things from Emmie. Next week was the Halloween party. She fell into a troubled sleep.

In the morning as she met Dorothy at the corner for the walk to school, Emmie wondered if she should tell her about what Mama said last night, but she just couldn't. Telling would make it seem more certain.

A chilly wind whistled out of the mountains. The girls walked faster and faster to get to the school, talking as they rushed along.

"The Halloween party's a basket social like last year, you know, Em. What are you going to bring?" Dorothy panted.

"What exactly is a basket social?" Emmie asked. "I

wasn't here last Halloween, remember?" She turned up the collar of her coat to keep out the cold.

"I forgot," Dorothy said. "It's seems like you've always been here—and we've always been best friends. What happens is that all the girls bring a lunch in a box or a basket. We call it a basket social, but some people bring a box if they don't have a basket. The lunch should be the best things you can think of, and it should have enough for two people to eat. You decorate up your basket or box as pretty as you can because they are all sitting up on a table together before they get picked.

"Then," she continued, shivering in the cold morning air, "here's the not so good part, but it's sort of fun too. No one is supposed to know whose basket is whose. But they do. The boys each get to choose a basket. My Mom said that at the grown-up basket socials, the men bid real money on the baskets, but not at the school one. Can you imagine Mr. McBean letting the boys bid real money?" She raised her eyebrows and made a face. "It's a miracle we even get to have the social. And we get to wear costumes too."

"What happens with the food in the baskets?" Emmie asked curiously. The costumes were no problem, but this basket social thing sounded unpredictable.

"You have to eat lunch with the boy that picks your basket. Last year we went by alphabet, but it didn't turn out too fair, so this year the teachers said they'd draw numbers."

"My lands!" Emmie exclaimed, borrowing a Lovelace expression. "You have to sit with them? And share? Whoever it is?"

"Right. Guess who I got last year? Acey! It was awful. He ate the dessert first and got chocolate cake crumbs all over the inside of my basket. Then he ate the sandwich—it was my Mom's good chicken salad. He yelled, 'Girlie chicken salad,' and made a face. Everybody laughed. He sure gobbled it up though. I was glad when it was over. Maybe this year, I'll get a better partner. Like Conrad."

They were at the school door. It was too cold to stop and talk any more.

"Thanks for telling me about it, Dorth." Emmie's teeth were chattering. "I'll take Acey for you this year," she grinned.

"Best friend forever," Dorothy replied.

By the end of the school day when Emmie walked in the door of the boarding house, thoughts about the basket, the costume, and the party competed with her worries.

Mama was at her desk again. She listened as Emmie told her everything Dorothy had said about the Basket Social. "We can search in the attic for something for your costume and maybe even a basket too. Ruth had many treasures up there."

"I've already thought of my costume, Mama," Emmie said. "I'm going to be Jeannette Rankin."

"That's quite an idea," Mama said. There was a hesitation in her response, but Emmie didn't notice it and chattered on.

"I could wear your hat and blouse and black skirt. A little bit like Miss Rankin looked at the Fair. It'll fit if I roll the skirt up at the waist. I'll wear my Votes for Women sash from the parade. I can put signs on my basket and…"

"Honey," Mama interrupted, "there is one thing I think we should think about."

She looked serious.

Emmie looked at Mama questioningly.

"You know," Mama went on. "Not everyone in Philipsburg thinks that women should vote. Some people do, but not everyone. The election will be held a few days after Halloween so there's lots of talk about it right now. I wouldn't want you to get your feelings hurt if some children have heard their parent's discussions and might say something against the women's vote."

"I wouldn't be surprised, Mama. No matter what they said. I already heard two boys say, 'Don't let the girls vote. They're too silly.' I don't care what they say. I want to be Miss Rankin. But Mama, why doesn't everybody think women should vote?" She plopped down beside Mama in the high backed chair by the desk.

"Sometimes when things change from the way they've always been, some people are afraid because they don't know what will happen. In Montana, men have been voting and choosing the leaders and making the decisions about laws and government since Montana became a state in 1889," Mama explained.

"There's just as many women and girls as the old boys." Emmie sat up straighter in the chair.

"That's true now, but at the start of the Montana territory, there were more men than women. Then, brave women came to our state and worked hard too," Mama continued. "Now it's way past time that we vote also. It will take a while for some people to get used to it though."

"Papa would want us to vote, wouldn't he, Mama?"

"He would be marching right with us."

"That does it. I will be Miss Rankin, and I won't care what anybody says."

Mama closed the ledger book and put the papers into the desk cubby holes. "Well, you're brave like Miss Rankin. You're smart and courageous like Miss Rankin. And," she patted Emmie's knee, "you're pretty like Miss Rankin. Miss Rankin you will be. But your hair," Mama said teasingly, "I don't remember Miss Rankin having braids." She gave Emmie's braid a gentle tug. "We'll do your hair up like Miss Rankin. She has beautiful thick hair like you do."

The night before the social, Mama served dinner early. Conrad and Nels pitched in to clean up the dishes and the kitchen so they would have a long evening to get everything ready. Conrad had decided to be an old prospector. Nels and Tom were outfitting him in torn trousers, a faded flannel shirt, a holey bandana, and a battered hat.

"For a finishing touch, smudge some dirt on your face on the way, son," Tom said.

"By tomorrow, there may not be any dirt to be found," Nels replied. "Look out this window."

Snow fell in thick fast flakes.

"Halloween snow," Emmie announced.

By morning, all of Philipsburg was covered in a deep blanket of white snow. Mama and Emmie made breakfast and Emmie's lunch for the social. Emmie had decided to take her lunch in a shoe box. She covered it in brown paper and cut a thin slot on the top. On the sides she had written BALLOT BOX in large black letters. She was Miss Rankin, and she would bring the ballot box.

She put apples, carrot sticks, sandwiches, and date bars made from Mama's special Hynes recipe in her box. She wasn't sure if anyone else would like the thick date bars made with chewy brown dates that came all the way from California in a package with a palm tree on it, but in the Hynes family, date bars rolled in powdered sugar were a special treat. Remembering Dorothy's story about the chicken salad comment last year, she put in a piece of candy too, just in case the date bars weren't popular.

"Could I also take an extra sandwich or two?" Emmie asked Mama as they cut up cold roast beef to place on thick soft slices of bread.

"Sure, but don't you think three of these big sandwiches will do? Your box is getting full."

"It's because of Clara," Emmie said. "I'm afraid she might not have anything for the social. Sometimes I share things from my lunch with her. She never brings very much food for lunch. Maybe I can take a box for her too."

"Of course. I didn't know you did that," Mama said, smiling.

Conrad came into the kitchen. "Danny too. Sometimes he only brings a cold potato sandwich wrapped in newspaper. It looks disgusting so I share my food."

Mama cut the bread for more sandwiches. "Oh, yes, we have plenty of bread and meat to share. I'm proud of you both for noticing."

After breakfast, Conrad and Emmie bundled up and headed out the front door. Mama watched them through the window as they tromped in the deep snow. They were laden down with the Ballot Box, an extra box for Clara, their school bags, and a knapsack Conrad took to make his costume complete. They looked like pack mules wading through the drifts.

By the time they got to the school, Mama's pinned up black skirt had come undone at the waist on one side and dragged along soaking wet from the snow. The Ballot Box was wet and the runny letters looked more like ALLO OX. But they'd made it, and everyone else came in the door all soggy too, stomping their feet to get off the clumps of snow.

In addition to the prospector accompanied by Jeannette Rankin, there was a beautiful, though damp, gypsy. Dorothy wore a black fringed shawl, a red flowered skirt, dangling beads, and an amazing sight—a bit of red tint on her lips.

"Dorth!" Emmie gasped. "You're beautiful."

Conrad was speechless.

Monte came in the room as a cowboy, complete with boots and spurs jangling as he kicked off the snow. One by one, the room filled with an assortment of costumed characters. Miss Moore greeted each one with a clap of her hands and exclaimed, "You look wonderful," even though some of them looked so bedraggled they were much less than wonderful.

Emmie glanced out the window to see a large white ghost trudging up to the school. She knew right away who it was. A wet sheet drooped over the ghost, who must have landed in a snowbank on the way. Emmie was glad she had brought the extra box of food.

As the soggy ghost came in the door, Emmie went over to it and whispered, "I have an extra box for the social for you, Clara."

"Thanks a lot, Emmie," murmured a muffled voice from beneath the sheet. "I couldn't find a box, and my Mama didn't have time to help me. I didn't want to cut holes in the sheet so I can't see anything."

When the bell rang, Miss Moore said, "Now class, we must try to get a little work done before the Basket Social at lunch time. Even cowboys, ghosts, gypsies, and famous ladies need to learn."

It seemed forever until lunchtime. When it finally arrived, everyone trooped into the big lunch room with a stage at one end. The baskets and boxes were put on a long table on the stage. It was wild chaos until Mr. Mc-Bean and Mrs. Featherly appeared.

"Children! Quiet!" Mr. McBean boomed out.

Mrs. Featherly countered Mr. McBean's startlingly loud un-party-like voice. "Now it is time for our Halloween Social, but not until you find your seats and settle down a bit," she said, waiting for the children to calm down. "When it's quiet, we will draw numbers for the lunches."

Everyone was hungry so it didn't take long until things quieted down.

This year's plan for the social was for the boys to draw numbers out of a hat and according to the numbers, choose the baskets they wanted, one by one. Nick U. said under his breath, "Finally! I might not be last in line for once." When the numbers were drawn, he was right. He was number three.

Mr. McBean stood on the stage by the table of baskets and boxes and announced, "Number one. Come up and pick a lunch."

The girls were nervous. Sharing lunch with a boy you

didn't want to sit with could be a disaster. But there was also the chance that someone like Monte M. might be your partner. Everyone was on the edge of their seats.

"Who is number one?" Mr. McBean inquired. Byron Anderson stood up, bounded up on stage, and picked a basket tied with green ribbons. A cluster of fifth grade girls giggled. A girl named Victoria stood up. Then Mr. McBean said, "Lunch partners number one. You can find a place at one of the tables." Byron and Victoria stiffly walked to a table but soon they were merrily unwrapping food from the basket.

After the first few numbers, the crowd grew more enthusiastic than scared, and there was cheering and giggling as the baskets were chosen and the partners revealed.

Finally, the number of baskets on the table dwindled down. The prospector had picked the gypsy's basket. They were happily digging into this year's chicken salad sandwiches. All around the room, the uncomfortable quiet had changed to a friendly hum of finding treats in the baskets.

About halfway through the picking process, Emmie had realized that her ink-stained ballot box was going to stay on the table for a long time. Acey even pointed at it and made a face when Mr. McBean wasn't looking. But she was resigned to wait and wait proudly, like Miss Rankin. When number after number was called, and no one picked the ALLO OX, she noticed that Monte

Montgomery was still sitting waiting to pick.

Finally, there were only four people waiting. Clara and Danny, Monte, and Jeannette Rankin. Danny and Clara were brother and sister. The situation had turned grim.

"Number twenty-five," Mr. McBean said.

"We're almost finished," Mrs. Featherly said in a too cheerful tone, trying to put a good light on the painful situation.

Monte walked up to the stage. On the table sat a plain box and the ballot box with the runny letters. Emmie's heart thumped. The spurs clanked as he walked up and picked the plain box. The ghost stood up and floated over to some seats left at a table.

Now Emmie just wanted to get to a table and get it over with, even if she had to eat with Danny. But right then, something happened to make it all right. Monte walked right by Emmie and gave her a wink. She knew he had picked Clara so a brother and sister didn't have to eat together. It was even better than sharing a lunch. She and Monte shared a secret.

Mr. McBean, in a rare moment of kindness, said, "Dan, you'll be eating with a famous young lady."

Danny picked up the lunch. "Yum," he said. During lunch he gobbled down two roast beef sandwiches, the fruit, the carrot sticks, and even the date bars, all without speaking or looking at Emmie.

After lunch, they played games, and Mr. McBean

told some scary stories. The party ended with bobbing for apples. Everybody had already gotten wet in the morning so they didn't mind putting their faces in the washtub of water with the bright red apples floating in it. One by one, they tried to sink their teeth into a bobbing apple. Their dripping faces come up from the surface, some victorious with an apple clenched in their teeth, and others gulping and laughing.

While the party was going on inside the warm school, outside it had been snowing all day. Before the usual time for school to get out, the teachers decided that the children should leave early before the snow piled any deeper.

Bundling into their coats, hats, scarves, and mittens, the children started out into the white world. They trudged off, hunched over to keep the driving snow from stinging their faces.

Emmie and Conrad came in the front door of the boarding house shaking the snow off. Mama helped unwrap the layers of clothes.

"This is a big snow," she exclaimed. "I'm glad the teachers let you out early. Tell me all about the party. Let's have some date bars and milk—or are you full from all the school treats?"

"Never full, Ma," Conrad grinned. "Especially after walking in this white stuff. I was dragging this gal." He gave Emmie a good natured tap.

"You were not," she said. "It's pretty deep though."

"Yes, Nels says that the roads to Anaconda and Butte are closed," Mama said.

As Emmie sat down at the kitchen table, her heart suddenly leaped for joy as she secretly thought, snow keep coming. Fill up the road to Butte and keep it closed all winter so we'll never be able to get back.

# Chapter Eleven

## Suffrage

November arrived on the calendar with dates of great importance. The day that suffrage would be voted on fell on November 3rd. The bank's deadline for the down payment loomed the next week.

On election day, snow was piled everywhere under a clear, cold, blue sky. People blinked when they stepped outside into the white snowy brightness.

Even though the day was sunny outside and filled with election possibilities, gray clouds hung inside the boarding house. The adding and re-adding of the ledger book could not make money where there was none. Mama did not have the money for the down payment. She had heard rumors that there were buyers waiting in the wings, just waiting for her deadline to come and go so they could buy the now much improved boarding house for themselves.

All of a sudden the catastrophe that had felt impossible was here, so close that they might be back in Butte before Christmas. Leaving Philipsburg, the boarding house, Old Nels, Dorothy, Monte, Miss Moore...it couldn't happen. But it was.

Emmie sat at her desk at school, staring out the window. Usually she listened to Miss Moore's every word, but today, her mind didn't focus. All she thought about was how to find a way to stay in Philipsburg, but no matter how hard she tried, she couldn't think of a way.

Miss Moore explained the election. "There are three levels being decided on," she said as she stood by the chalk board. "There is the local level. These are things that are decided for Philipsburg. Does anyone have an example of local issues?"

A hand shot up. When Miss Moore called on him, Douglas Flint said seriously, "The Sheriff."

"Good. That's right, Douglas." Miss Moore wrote his answer under LOCAL on the board. "And an example of a state matter?" She wrote STATE in large letters.

Not to be outdone by his brother, Jack Flint's hand waved in the air.

"Yes, Jack?" Miss Moore smiled at his eagerness.

"Woman Suffrage," Jack announced.

"Correct. The word suffrage means the right to vote in elections. This election will decide on allowing women to vote." She wrote SUFFRAGE on the board under STATE.

A funny sound came from the row by the windows.

"Acey, did you have something to say?" Miss Moore looked sternly at him.

"No, Ma'am. Just sneezing," Acey mumbled. But everyone knew it wasn't a sneeze and so did Miss Moore.

"Any disrespectful comments on this discussion and I will call Mr. McBean," she said.

Acey slumped in his seat.

"The last category is?"

"Federal." It was Clara.

Miss Moore looked happy that Clara had answered. "Yes indeed. Very good," she beamed at Clara. "Federal means matters affecting the whole United States and electing officials to serve the entire country such as…"

She paused and waited, the chalk poised in her hand by the board. A sea of hands waved in the air. "Everyone?"

"Congress and the President of the United States," said a chorus of voices.

"Yes. So there we have it. Citizens vote on local, state, and federal matters."

Though she usually joined in, today Emmie couldn't. Not with so many things on her mind. When school got out, she walked home with Dorothy as usual.

"You're kind of quiet today, Em," Dorothy said.

"I guess so," Emmie replied. "I'm worried about my Mom and some things."

"Can I help you? You know I would," Dorothy looked at Emmie sympathetically.

"I know you would, Dorth," Emmie said. All of a sudden, she couldn't hold back the news any longer. Her voice came out in short jerky breaths. "We have to move back to Butte. I didn't tell you about it before because I kept hoping it wouldn't happen. But now that Auntie Ruthie is gone, we have to pay a giant lump of money to the bank to buy the boarding house. We don't have the money and now the bank will sell the boarding house to someone else. We have to move back to Butte." Her eyes welled up with tears.

"No, Em!" Dorothy's face was shocked. She stopped right in her tracks. "You can't leave. It can't be true."

Emmie looked sad. They were both shivering. "I don't know when, but soon. It's awful."

Dorothy moaned, "I'd do anything to help you." She put her arm around Emmie.

"I'll tell you more later, but it's true. It's getting cold now though. Maybe we'd better get home," Emmie said quietly.

They started walking, their heads down dejectedly. People bustled along the street toward the Granite County Courthouse to vote, but Emmie and Dorothy didn't notice them.

When it came time to go their separate ways, they hugged each other in shivery, hopeless silence. Dorothy said, "I'll ask my Mom if I can come see you after I get my homework done. We could talk more then. I'm supposed to help get ready for our party if suffrage passes, but this is way more important."

Emmie nodded distractedly. She'd forgotten all about the party. A party couldn't help them now.

The table was quiet that night at dinner as a steaming bowl of rich brown beef stew with carrots and potatoes was passed around.

Old Nels spoke up first. "I hope everybody voted today," he announced. He brought a faint smile to Mama's worried face when he said, "Someone who works as hard as you do, Honora Hynes, deserves to have the right to vote." That was all he said, but everyone at the table knew exactly how he had voted.

Tom Beam raised his coffee cup in the air. "Hear, hear," he pronounced. "At least that's two votes for Granite County."

While they were doing the dishes that night, Mama said that she would get out some boxes tomorrow so they could begin packing up. She said that she would tell the boarders soon. It seemed as though even Mama was putting things off day by day in the desperate hope that a miracle would reverse their fate. But the deadline for the payment was here, the house would be sold, and they'd be gone.

When the votes were counted all over Montana and they heard the news, it was a glorious YES for woman suffrage. It was a close vote and not every county had voted yes, but it didn't matter because enough people had voted yes. At last, Montana women could vote.

A grand celebration would be held on Saturday at the Lovelace's. Dorothy described the preparations to Emmie on the way to school, but neither of them felt excited. Each day brought them closer to the move and they knew it.

On Saturday morning as Mama and Emmie cleared the breakfast dishes, Emmie said, "Dorothy asked me to come over early to help set things up for the party today. Could I?"

"Yes, Em." Mama's reply didn't have any party enthusiasm in it.

"The election is great news, isn't it, Mama?" She wanted so much to cheer her Mama up. "Aren't you happy about it?"

"I am," Mama said. She sat down wearily and reached for her flowered coffee cup. "Let's take a little break."

It was the serious-talking Mama looking at Emmie. "The election news is good," Mama said. "So many people worked hard for this, and now we will finally move forward. It's bigger than just voting in one election or for one person. I think you're old enough to understand this. The way things are done in a bigger way can change too."

She paused and took a sip of her coffee. "Our troubles are things that could be helped by better laws. When Papa died, it was an accident. He wasn't doing anything wrong. Because he worked at the mines, the mining company should have helped us with money after he died. But they didn't because there was no law to make them do what was right.

Our help came from the Union of workers that

Papa had worked with, from the Irish Society that helps Irish people, from what Papa had saved for us, and from what friends gave to us because Papa was so generous in helping other people when they needed it. It was wonderful help, given with kindness from people's hearts. Even people who couldn't afford to helped us. People I didn't even know came to me with little bits of money and said that Papa had helped them once so they wanted to help us.

All that kindness got us to Philipsburg. But there wasn't one bit of help from the mining company. They only wanted to keep all their profits for themselves. That is why laws are needed to make the companies do what is right for their workers, so other families won't have the same trouble we're having. Voting for fair laws is worth fighting for with all your strength."

"I understand it, Mama."

Mama sighed, as if she could barely speak the next words. "There is one thing we could do. We need to think about it real hard. I could ask the Lovelace family if you could stay with them for the rest of this school year. Conrad might be able to stay with Montgomery family. Then you wouldn't have to leave Philipsburg. I could go back to Butte by myself and work."

"NO, Mama." Emmie moved onto her Mama's lap, her long legs dangling to the floor, her head buried in Mama's shoulder. "Never. We have to stay together. We're a family. I think Conrad feels the same."

"He does," Conrad said. They hadn't seen him, but he'd been standing at the kitchen door. "We stay together, Mama."

"Come here, son," Mama reached out to him.

They didn't speak. Words wouldn't help. They were leaving, and they all knew it.

Finally, Mama broke the stillness. "I love you children more than anything in the world." Her voice cracked, but she regained herself. "Now we will go to the party to celebrate."

"They'll have lots of good food," Emmie said, but her voice sounded flat.

"Now I must tell you both some other things too," Mama said. It was as if once the subject was out in the air, Mama was going to plow through it to the end.

"I will tell the boarders. I'm sure they may not be too surprised. I wanted to wait until things were definite. I don't know what the new owners will be like, but it will affect the boarders." Mama was businesslike now. "They'll need to begin planning."

Emmie's stomach churned. She wanted to act grown-up, but she felt scared and small. She didn't feel at all like a party, but after chores, she halfheartedly got ready to go up to Dorothy's. Mama and Conrad would walk up the hill to the Lovelace's big brick house later.

Emmie and Dorothy filled the candy and nut dishes and arranged plates on the tables. For a little while, in the anticipation and atmosphere of getting ready for the party, Emmie almost forgot her troubles.

Soon the doorbell rang. The Lovelace's parlor and dining room began to fill with people. The Votes for Women banners from the parade hung around the room. The polished, curving staircase leading upstairs to Dorothy's bedroom was wrapped in yellow and gold ribbons. Guests squeezed into every corner of the rooms, ladies proudly wearing their Votes for Women buttons and gentlemen in suits with buttons on their lapels. Grey clouds filled the wide sky outside and out across the white fields of Flint Creek valley to the distant mountains. Inside, a warm welcome greeted the celebrating citizens.

As Emmie helped Dorothy refill a tray of sweets, she heard Mr. Lovelace open the front door and say hello to Mama and Conrad. Emmie wiggled her way through the crowd to reach them. She wanted to stick right by her Mama today.

Mr. Lovelace took Mama's coat and hat. "It's a great time for Montana," he boomed. From across the room, Mrs. Lovelace motioned to Mama to join her with a group of friends. Mama, Conrad, and Emmie stepped into the sea of celebration, trying to look as if they were in a party mood.

Each time the doorbell rang, the crowd expanded to squeeze in new guests. People held china dishes filled with treats, and balanced plates on their laps. There were cookies and cakes, small sandwiches, and chocolates arranged on sparkling glass trays. The grownups' champagne bubbled in long stemmed glasses. The children dipped punch from a glass bowl into little cups.

Mr. and Mrs. Montgomery were talking to them when all of a sudden there was another outburst of exclamations at the front door. A tall man stood in the foyer, shaking snow off his hat and slapping his leather gloves together. It was Mr. George, the lawyer from Butte.

Mr. Lovelace greeted him. "Will George. You drove all the way from Butte? We didn't think you'd make it."

"I couldn't miss this party," Mr. George said, "but I may have to stay all winter. It looks like more snow tonight."

The party flowed on cheerfully with congratulatory speeches and the din of friendly conversation, but it wasn't too long before Mama gathered the children and said they must be going. Mama didn't seem to be able to focus on a party at all.

After proper good byes, they stepped carefully off the icy steps and walked down the snowy hill toward Broadway Street and home—the boarding house, their boarding house. During the party, Emmie had tried to forget her worries, but now, as the dusk fell around them, the troubles came right back and seemed even worse. Emmie glanced at the Lovelaces' big house with all its lights on and the glow of the party reflected through the windows. Her heart sank again at the thought of leaving all this behind. It was cold as they walked along quietly.

# Chapter Twelve

## Thanksgiving

"Mr. George is coming over later," Mama said after their Sunday noon meal. "But now, I am going to work on packing. With this weather, when an opportunity comes for a ride to Butte, we may have to be ready at the spur of the moment."

When Mama went upstairs, a thought hit Emmie like a bolt. Could it be that they'd have to go back to Butte with Mr. George, she worried. Right now?

Conrad was half-heartedly doing his homework. "No matter what I write, I can't please old Bean. Who cares anyway?" He put down his pencil.

Emmie closed her book and looked at him desperately. "What are we going to do?"

"I don't know, Em. I've tried every which way to think of something. Everything's a dead end. I guess we're leaving. I can't believe it though."

"Me neither," Emmie said. "If only…"

"If only what?" Conrad replied. "There don't seem to be any 'if only's' left."

"I don't think Mama has told the boarders," Emmie

said, holding her head in her hands. "But they must have seen the boxes."

"Have you told anybody?" Conrad asked.

"Just Dorothy," Emmie replied. "I kept hoping maybe it won't be true."

"This is no maybe, Em." Conrad's lips were a grim line.

Emmie swallowed hard. "I think we should tell Nels. And tell other people too—to make it easier for Mama. It's just too hard for her to admit it. Maybe if we tell, it will help her."

"Okay, Em. I think you're right."

Later that afternoon, when Mama and Mr. George were talking in the parlor, Emmie and Conrad knocked on Nels's bedroom door.

"Come in." Nels sat in his big chair, reading a newspaper and smoking his pipe.

The story poured out of Emmie and Conrad. Nels's room was plain and sparse, with a few of his own touches like a Swedish flag draped over a trunk, a faded quilt on the bed, and a postcard of a lake in Sweden pinned on the wall.

"I knew something was wrong," Nels said seriously. "Your Mama has not been herself lately. I'm glad you told me. Now we must get to work."

"Yes, awful work," Emmie blurted out. "Mama says we have to start packing,"

"I will tell Tom myself. Let's not tell the other boarders quite yet," Nels said. He didn't look as upset as Emmie thought he might.

"Thank you." Conrad stood up.

"No, it's me thanking you, son. I will see you at supper. I won't let on about what we've talked about."

Emmie didn't feel at all right, not telling Mama about their talk with Nels. She felt badly that they'd gone behind Mama's back, but she hoped maybe they were helping her too. At least now someone knew that it was only a matter of time.

At supper, not a word more was said. Nels and Tom came into the dining room together. Tom said, "Hello, you hooligans," very cheerily.

Nels must not have told him, Emmie thought. Tom's good cheer almost made her mad.

"Nice to see Will George in town," Nels said when they were finishing eating. "He is a fine man."

"With the trouble in the mines in Butte, Will George is a good voice for the miners," Tom said.

"Union trouble," another boarder said, and the conversation took on a serious grown-up tone.

"Please clear the table, children," Mama motioned to Emmie and Conrad. Emmie knew why. No conversation for children. That was okay. They both had things to talk about too.

In the kitchen, Emmie whispered to Conrad, "Do you think we'll have to drive back to Butte with Mr. George? I'm scared. Maybe we'd better tell Mama that we told Nels too. Why do you think he doesn't seem sad?" Emmie peppered Conrad with questions.

"I don't know the answers, Em," he said, shaking his head. "I think it's okay we told though. I'll tell Mont and Bobby too, but not Danny. He'd just say it would be good to go back to Butte. I have to finish my homework now though. Probably it doesn't matter, but if I show up tomorrow without it, I'll be too dead to move back to Butte."

The next day at school when Miss Moore called on Emmie and Dorothy, they both gave short answers, but something was very different. The day crawled along until Emmie got home from school. Mama was upstairs in her room. The sight of boxes in front of Mama's closet made Emmie's heart sink. She slumped onto the bed.

"Mama, Conrad and I told Nels about moving. I told Dorothy too." She blurted out. "We told to help you. So you wouldn't have to."

Mama sat down by Emmie on the bed. "It's all right," she said softly. "I'm telling people myself too. It's hard to admit it, I guess. I wanted so much to make this work." Mama looked about eleven years old too.

"You did everything you could, Mama. You did make it work for us. We'll be okay. Maybe we'll come back. We can do it. We'll be together."

Right that minute, Emmie would have said or done anything in the world to try and help her Mama. Pack the boxes. Move to Butte. Put up with mean old Uncle Henry. Find a job. Get some money. And somehow, someway, get back to Philipsburg.

All of a sudden, she didn't feel quite so helpless. It was the same fight-back power that she'd found in the fight with Clara. She didn't know where it came from, but here it was, and she was determined.

"We will be fine, Mama," she said quietly.

"Thank you," Mama whispered back.

They sat for a while longer until Mama said, "Let's leave the packing for now and start dinner."

Dinner was a big pan of cheesy potatoes with spicy sausage. While it bubbled baking in the oven, Emmie stirred the green beans they had canned last summer. The table was set for the boarders, but no one was there by six o'clock. They were late from work.

While they were cooking dinner, Mama told Emmie that she had decided to tell the boarders about the change in ownership at dinner. She seemed nervous when everyone was late. Emmie felt nervous too. Even Nels and Tom weren't home yet. The potatoes grew browner and browner in the oven.

Finally, one by one, the boarders came in the front door and went upstairs to wash up for dinner. At last everyone was seated around the table, passing the food, and filling their plates. Usually the boarders carried on some conversation during dinner, and Mama and Emmie made sure there was plenty of food.

Tonight neither Mama nor Emmie had much appetite. Their plates were hardly touched.

As the men finished eating and leaned back from the table, Mama cleared her throat. "There is something I must tell you all."

Everyone looked up, but before she said anything more, Old Nels spoke. "There is something we must tell you too. You don't need to tell us about the boarding house problems. Two messengers have seen to that." He glanced at Emmie and Conrad. "It is good they have, because we have had a meeting and we all agree that we can work extra hours to pay you more rent and..."

Mama, who would normally never interrupt anybody, just couldn't stop talking. She was so intent on making everything clear to the boarders that she interrupted Nels and launched into the words that she must have been rehearsing all afternoon in her mind.

"I appreciate that, but I'm afraid there is much more to it than the rent. As you know, the bank has settled Ruth Davies's estate. I'd hoped to be able to buy the boarding house myself. I'd hoped for a settlement from the mining company so I could make a down payment on the house, but I have not been able to gather that money."

Emmie glanced at the faces around the table. All eyes were fixed on Mama.

"The bank gave me a generous amount of time to accumulate the down payment, but now their deadline for me is here. I do not have the money and the boarding house will be sold to another buyer."

Mama shook her head sadly. "It is kind of you to offer to pay more rent, but I'm afraid that will not help. I'm so sorry."

Nels and Tom glanced at each other and Nels seemed to want to speak again, but no one could get a word in edgewise as Mama continued, one word piling on another so she would not mislead the boarders.

"I hope that the boarding house will stay open and you will be able to pay the same rent. But for me and the children, the future is uncertain. I have made plans for us to move back to Butte."

She slumped back in her chair. She seemed relieved that everyone knew the whole situation at last. Emmie and Conrad watched the serious faces around the table. The eyes of every boarder, rough miners, and cowboys, familiar friends, and new guests, were all focused on Mama. Nels nodded at Tom Beam and then began to speak.

"We have all watched you working so hard, Mrs. Hynes. Because of you, this boarding house is not just a place for us to sleep. It's a home. The bankers want a big down payment because they think you're running a business, but what they don't know is that you're really running a family—this family, all of us. You and the children belong here. Now it is our turn to help you."

Mama smiled weakly, but she still looked hopeless.

Tom Beam rose from his chair and cleared his gruff

voice. He pulled a crumpled piece of paper from his shirt pocket. "Here is something to help. Me and Nels have a little stash of money from an old mining claim up in them hills by Granite. We always thought we'd save it for a rainy day, but, if you ask me, right now it's raining cats and dogs."

He passed the crumpled mine claim paper around the table. "This is a nice amount. Added to your savings, Mrs. Hynes, it will put you...us...over the top for the down payment. Please accept it so these doors can stay open, and we can all stay a good long time." He chuckled. "Won't those old geezers at the bank be surprised when we show up tomorrow with a down payment?"

Relieved smiles eased the faces of everyone around the table. Mama looked stunned. She looked first at Nels, then at Tom, and they both nodded in agreement. She tried to gather herself together, but finally she pulled up her apron and just buried her face in it. When she peeked out from the cloth, she was crying.

Emmie didn't take her eyes off Mama. She had to know. Was it too good to be true? Would they really be able to stay? "Can we?" Emmie mouthed the words.

Mama nodded. This time Mama's tears didn't make Emmie feel sad, or scared, or helpless, or anything but happy.

Nels rose from his place and came to stand behind Emmie. "Yes, it's true, little one," he said, putting his hand on her shoulder. "We will all stay. Together."

It was Emmie who was finally able to say their thank you when she and Conrad stood at the end of the table, hugging their Mama, surrounded by Nels, Tom, and a table full of boarders—their family.

Conrad shook hands with Nels and Tom as Emmie said, "Unpack those boxes, Mama. We just need a tiny bit more money—to buy a great big turkey, because we're going to have the best Thanksgiving ever."

# Afterword

## A Note from Emmie: Philipsburg, Montana, June, 1915

That's the story of our amazing P'burg year. (We can call it P'burg like the old timers do cuz now we're old timers too.) I'm twelve and Conrad's thirteen. He and Dorothy are still stuck on each other. But I guess I can't talk. School just got out for the summer. Even though I'm glad it's summer vacation, I sure will miss having Monte Montgomery right across the aisle. Next year, we'll move upstairs to Mr. McBean. It'll be hold-on-to-your-hat time up there.

Our boarding house is always filled to bursting. Every room. We could probably even rent out the parlor. Mama is still working to get the money from the mine bosses and Mr. George still comes over from Butte. It's warmer now. We've put up the porch swing again.

Mama's birthday is coming soon. I don't know why I can never get started on a present for her until the very last minute. I'll think of something though. At least Conrad won't try that fight stunt again this year. He'd better not. All in all, he's a pretty good brother, even if he does act all google-eyed around Dorothy. This year I'll make the cake from Auntie Ruthie's recipe.

*Not one day goes by that I don't think of my Papa. I sure do miss him. I guess I always will. Yesterday, a man from Butte came to our boarding house to rent a room for a few nights. Mama was down at the store so I showed him around, and he said to me, "Are you John Hynes' daughter, from Butte?"*

*Those words sounded like music to me. "Yes, I am," I said. "I'm Emmie Hynes, and now I'm from Butte and Philipsburg, Montana." When I said that, I knew in my heart that it would carry me a long, long way.*

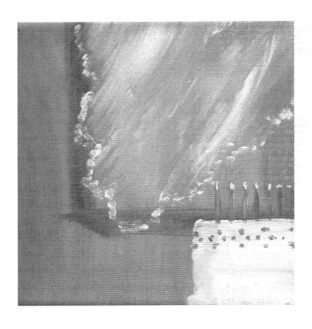

# Acknowledgements

All thanks go to all my family members and friends who read this manuscript, helped with ideas, words, and pictures; understood, encouraged, and gently cheered for Mama, Conrad, and Emmie.

Especially to Steve, Courtney, Nick, Colin, Doug, and Jack

Thank you to the families who were my inspiration for this story: the Lovinger, Melton, Hynes, and Hokanson families.

Special thanks to Fran for her art, Jeanette for the thoughtful questions, and to the Pony Writing Group for their encouragement.

And especially to Janet Muirhead Hill and Florence Ore without whom the Boarding House doors would never have opened again in 2012.

# A Raven Publishing Guide
## For Classroom and Reading Group Discussion
by Jeanette Daane

1. The title and setting for the story is a boarding house. Have you known anyone who has lived in a boarding house? Why do you think people may not live at boarding houses in modern times? Do you think it might be fun to live at a boarding house? Why or why not?

2. In the prologue, Emmie gives the reader "a note" to explain her determination to help Mama in the face of the change in their lives. What are the qualities you see in Emmie as the story proceeds that enable her to be of help?

3. Conrad struggles with the changes in their lives. At what times does he have trouble, and at what times does he show strength?

4. In the very first sentence, we learn that Papa died working in the Butte mines. Yet we get to know him, mainly through the memories and actions of his family. What did you learn about Papa? What are some of the things you might have liked about him?

5. How is Philipsburg different from Butte?

6. For a brief moment in the fight scene (Chapter One) Emmie experiences the thrill of a well placed punch to Clara. She is able to see that fighting can change a person. What might some of these changes be? What were Old Nels's words about fighting?

7. Danny and Clara are characters in the story who make the reader feel both anger and sympathy. How do you feel about Danny and Clara? Without a description of their home, how would you imagine it? What are clues to the life of Danny and Clara? Do you think that Emmie and Clara become friends?

8. Birthday parties seem to have similarities in all periods of time. In what ways did the party for Mama resemble modern birthday parties, and in what ways was it different?

9. Why was Mama's birthday party and her gift of such importance to Emmie? Emmie's gift of an apron is unusual for today. Why were aprons a common part of women's clothing in those times? Why do you think they are worn less often now?

10. The Model T Ford that Belle and Auntie Ruth drive, also called the Tin Lizzie, was a surprisingly sturdy automobile. Henry Ford said customers could have any paint color they wanted so long as it was black. Have you seen a Model T Ford at a classic car show or at a museum? Did you see how it was started? Can you picture the two women in an open air car driving the roads of Montana?

11. In Montana, copper, gold and silver were and still are mined. What makes copper mining dangerous? Why did men continue to work in those mines?

12. In chapter five, we see Conrad's strength come through. In what ways does he show maturity and courage?

13. Emmie attends funerals for Papa and then for Auntie Ruth. She has thoughts about the services. Do you agree with her conclusion or do you have a different opinion on church customs at the time of a funeral? Are the children and the adults handling grief differently?

14. In Chapter Seven, Emmie uses simile and metaphor to describe Dorothy and herself on the first day of school. She pictures them as food. Dorothy is peaches and cream. Emmie is apple cobbler with cinnamon. Have you ever thought of yourself or someone else in terms of food? What food would you be? What food would a friend or family member be? Besides food, what other kinds of similes could be used for describing people?

15. In what ways would the school in Philipsburg be different from most schools today? What was surprising to Emmie and Dorothy about the new teacher, Miss Moore?

16. Emmie is surprised and puzzled by the message on the chalkboard: "Teachers open the doors. You enter by yourself." What do you think this Chinese proverb means? Why would a teacher put it on the board for all the students?

17. Emmie's mother explains some of the reasons why people were opposed to suffrage for women. Can you think of other reasons people might have had to object to women voting?

18. Conditions of mines and financial provisions for accidents were unregulated and without rules to govern the

employers' actions. What could have changed this situation? Do you think the vote of women may have made the difference? Why?

19. Jeannette Rankin was inspiring to the people of the time. She became the first woman in Congress, elected in 1916 and again in 1940. The story doesn't cover her life in Washington but do you happen to know what vote in both terms set her apart from the rest of the Congress? It might be interesting for you to look this up.

20. Have you been to a basket or box social? Was it similar to the one at Emmie's school? Emmie likes Monte, but she is especially impressed by what he does at the school's box social. What does he do that makes her like him even more?

21. Were you surprised at how Mama was able to keep the boarding house? Did you expect the mining company to help her? Why do you think the boarders wanted to help her? There is an old quote that says, "A family is where you find it." Does this quote apply to this story?

22. The Boarding House is the title of this book. In some ways, the house is a "character" in the book. Is it possible for non-human things to be used as characters in a story? What are some examples from other books you may have read? Describe the boarding house as a character. What are its qualities?

23. Not all books have a prologue and an afterword. What do you think the author's purpose was in using them in

this book? In whose point of view (voice) are the prologue and afterword told? How is this different from the body of the story? What affect did this have on you as a reader?

24. After reading the afterword, what do you think Emmie and Conrad learned during their P'burg year? What do you imagine might happen next for the characters in this book. See if you can make up a "next chapter" for them.

25. What are some of the themes that you find in this book? Can you think of other books that address the same themes?

*Jeannette Rankin speaking from the balcony of the National American Woman Suffrage Association building in Washington D.C. (circa 1917)*

*Photo courtesy of the Montana Historical Society*

## Suggested Books for Young Readers

More reading and photos of the Montana history, places, and people mentioned in this story.

**Butte's Pride: The Columbia Gardens**, by Pat Kearney. Butte, MT: Skyhigh Comm., 1994.

**Butte's Memory Book.** Caldwell ID: Caxton Printers, 1975.

**Images of America: Butte**, by Ellen Crain and Lee Whitney. Charleston, SC: Arcadia, 2009.

**Jeannette Rankin: Bright Star in the Big Sky**, by Mary Barmeyer O'Brien. Helena, MT: Falcon, 1995.

**Jeannette Rankin: First Lady of Congress**, by Trish Marx. New York: Margaret K. McElderry Books, 2006.

**Jeannette Rankin: Political Pioneer**, by Gretchen Woelfle. Honesdale, PA: Boyds Mills, 2007.

**Montana: Stories of the Land**, by Krys Holmes. Helena, MT: Montana Historical Society Press, 2008.

**More Than Petticoats: Remarkable Montana Women**, by Gayle C. Shirley. Helena, MT: Falcon, 1995.

**A Voice from the Wilderness: The Story of Anna Howard Shaw**, by Don Brown. Boston: Houghton Mifflin, 2001.